The Girl with the
Full Figure Is Your Daughter

The Girl with the Full Figure Is Your Daughter

by Oscar Martens

TURNSTONE PRESS

Turnstone Press
607-100 Arthur Street
Artspace Building
Winnipeg, MB
R3B 1H3 Canada
www.TurnstonePress.com

Turnstone Press gratefully acknowledges the assistance of The
Canada Council for the Arts, the Manitoba Arts Council, the Government of
Canada through the Book Publishing Industry Development Program
and the Government of Manitoba through the Department of Culture,
Heritage and Tourism, Arts Branch for our publishing activities.

    Canadä

Cover design: Tétro Design
Interior design: Sharon Caseburg
Author photograph: Seth Berkowitz
Printed and bound in Canada by Friesens for Turnstone Press.

National Library of Canada Cataloguing in Publication Data

Martens, Oscar, 1968-
    The girl with the full figure is your daughter / Oscar Martens.

Short stories.

ISBN 0-88801-272-1

    I. Title.

PS8576.A7654G47 2002   C813'.6   C2002-903269-5

PR9199.4.M27G47 2002

For close friends and careful readers,
Stacy Ashton, Lynn Forbes, and Wayne Jones.

Acknowledgements

For their encouragement and suggestions over the years, I would like to thank da Group, Peter Hilborne, James Spyker, Steven Heighton, David Arnason, Rita Donovan, Nadine McInnis, John Barton, Gabriella Goliger, and Paul McKeague. I am grateful to Wayne Tefs, my editor, for his patient, gentle guidance. Thanks to the journals that found room for my work, especially *Event*, *PRISM international*, and *Prairie Fire*. Lastly, I would like to thank the helpful and supportive people at Turnstone Press.

Contents

The Girl with the Full Figure Is Your Daughter

The Girl with the Full Figure Is Your Daughter

My father's place is cold, he lives like a slob and I really don't want to be here. I always get a sore throat, sometimes before I'm even in his apartment. That makes as much sense as standing in the hallway in front of his door with my stomach clenched while the plastic handles from the grocery bags cut off blood from my fingers.

I have many ways to explain the tension. Arthur, my father, seems to be getting worse. He writes notes on index cards and leaves them around the apartment so he can remember things. My job is to determine his level of functioning and compensate for the lack of it. I might be the one who decides he can no longer live on his own.

It stinks inside. It's hard to find room on the kitchen counter where I can set down the groceries. The dishes that aren't mouldy have dried food stuck to them. The TV is on and there are porn magazines laid out on the couch. A pair of dirty underwear hangs off one of the arms of the recliner.

you are trying to reduce your intake of fats and sugars

Using my new method of cleaning, I walk around with an orange hefty bag and throw out anything that is objectionable. And I've bought rubber gloves so I don't actually have to touch anything. I trust his forgetfulness not to miss these things and his sense of shame not to mention them if he notices. I don't know if this is evil or not. It probably is.

Arthur sputters whenever I talk about moving him to a nicer place, a place where he can be cared for properly. He tells me I should take care of him properly and then he would be happy. Arthur wishes I would be like his wife who was a *real* woman. Comments like that make me realize that if it weren't for the weekly doses of intimidation and shame from Cal, I would have written off Arthur long ago.

you were a union organizer until may 18, 1978

Arthur walks in naked again. It doesn't matter how many times I tell him. I see him in my peripheral vision, but I can't face him. We play this scene one more time. I skirt the perimeter of the room until I can make it to the bathroom to get a towel to put around his waist. Sometimes he blocks the way to the bathroom.

I can't do it today. I have the towel, but I can't put it around his waist. I can barely stand the smell of him. I hold out the towel and tell him to put it on. He ignores me. I order him to do it, almost growling out the words.

He finally puts it on and sits down to watch TV. Today, lesbians who have battled both sexism and prejudice to become ministers in the church.

the rent is due on the last day of every month

I vacuum around him. I dust around him. I send his filth

down the garbage chute. His cards seem to be breeding. I try to put them in places where they will be most helpful. The people ones go by the phone, the diet ones near the fridge and so on. There's a new one on top of his radio in the bedroom:

the girl with the full figure is your daughter

My throat begins to throb. I search for a reason for my sudden anger. Arthur bumps into me from behind and then I'm staring at the cover over the ceiling light from my room in our old house.

There were two sockets but only one worked. A dim forty-watt bulb lit the room. I had studied it so closely, all the frilly designs etched into it and that pile of dead bugs darkening the centre.

I remember a big mayfly, hearing that zapping sound as it hit the light, maimed but not dead. I could see the shape of its body through the cover. It twitched for a while and I imagined myself in that strange glass bowl with the savage electric flame leaving me too weak to escape, roasting me.

When I sit down, Arthur sits beside me setting the right side of my body on fire. I have to move. Make tea. I have to make tea, find the kettle in the kitchen where it is cooler. I have to search for a tea bag but when I find one I just stand there squishing it, sweat from my fist mixing with the tea, staining me.

I leave Arthur's apartment and catch a bus on Hastings which is strange because I drove here. It's a few blocks before I've realized what I've done. A guy offers me his seat and it makes me want to kick him in the balls. This isn't even the right bus. It's an express and it won't stop until Brentwood Mall so I'm committed to a forty-five-minute bus ride in the wrong direction.

I'm going to get home eventually and when I do I'm going to set all the locks, pull the blinds and moan quietly into my pillow. For days, if necessary. Everybody is looking at me because they all know how dirty and useless I am.

I'm in the apartment before I can afford to think of it again. Simply this: looking up at the light cover while he did things. Then later, looking up at the cover while he did things and his penis was in my mouth. Choking me. Making me sticky. Later, his lecture on becoming a woman.

Memory hurts. Without it, I can function. With it, I'm lying here gasping for air. What's the point then? With more knowledge I am less able.

There's a tree on East Georgia that I can't go past anymore because the branches are shaped liked erect penises and when the wind blows they bob and dangle like the real thing. It's so rude I don't see how people can have that on their lawns. Why don't people run screaming?

And I'm fixated on microphones now so that eliminates any kind of concert or lecture. I can't go to the Malcolm Lowry Room on Wednesdays anymore. That's ruined for me. But worst of all is the men around me, men I used to trust, relationships I used to find appropriate and now I just don't know. There is no one who can guide me.

I wish I could go back in time to last month, before that tiny nut of information in my brain cracked open and poisoned everything. I was happy before. At least I think I was happy, which is the same thing.

I can't go back to his apartment now. That seems impossible. One night Cal calls me and starts scolding me for avoiding Arthur. He says if he were here he would handle it himself. He wonders if I can do anything right. He forces me to promise to visit Arthur.

It takes three weeks to get to the point where I can stand stupidly in front of this door again. How can it be possible that I have returned to do kind things for Arthur? What is wrong with me that I am able to do this?

Arthur's out, thank god. I see why he requested extra cards.

They're all over the apartment by now. There's guilt as I think of him alone for three weeks followed by anger for feeling guilt.

Among the cards on the table there is an incomplete one that says *you have*. I finish it for him, easily imitating his wobbly scrawl. I reach for a blank card. After twenty I plan to mix them with his cards but it seems better to collect his and throw them out. An hour later, I have replaced all of his cards with my versions.

you have no real worth

Cal phones three days later. Something is wrong with our father. Arthur's really shaken about something but he doesn't know what. Cal said Arthur sounded confused and hurt and close to tears.

you will always be alone

I think this is beautiful while I try to choose the correct response for a loving daughter. Cal might hear my smile if I'm not careful when I speak. He's flying out from Calgary on the weekend. My stomach clenches as I think of ways to prepare for his arrival.

you will be punished for what you have done

Everything I can remember goes into my notes, all the things that happened to me, with approximate dates. It's a heavy thing, this feeling of doom, but I'm hoping a script will prevent me from feeling like a child. If I don't have one they'll just roll over me. I'll start crying or become weak.

Cal is worse in person. It's only on the phone that I can distance myself from his insults and belittling. He's a small man with wound-up tension that makes him seem close to violence. Wrinkles that might make other men look wise and gentle make him fierce and severe.

When I open the door to Arthur's apartment, Cal steams toward me with all his force and anger. He holds up a pair of Arthur's underwear and yells at me for the place being such a mess. There is crap everywhere but no more than usual. Cal wants to know how this is possible. Don't I care about our father? How is Arthur supposed to be happy in a mess like this? I have a lot of explaining to do.

I say I will be happy to explain everything and ask them to sit down. My hand is in my purse, gripping my notes. I have been so scared of losing them, or Arthur destroying them, that I made a copy and mailed it to myself.

As I pull out my papers, they sit on opposite ends of the couch, suspicious of what I am doing, impatient for me to start. The notes probably make me look ridiculous but I start reading anyway, without looking up. When I'm finished I wait for a response.

Cal grabs my notes and asks if I've been spending all this time writing short stories, all this time, leaving poor Arthur on his own so I could practise creative writing. And it's not even very good writing. And why would I want to write about some disgusting thing like that? Why would I want to make up all those horrible things about my father?

Arthur calls me crazy, wonders if that's what an education does for you, makes you crazy, makes you talk trash to your father. Cal won't let me have my notes back, holding them above his head as I try to reach them. I'm getting flashes of scenes from a homicide, yellow tape covering the door.

I go for the old suitcase under Arthur's bed because Cal has to know what a sick fucker this old guy is with his mountains of porn. There's some kiddie stuff in here, I know it. I'd like to see Arthur explain that away. There's so much of it in the old case and most of it's new. This isn't a classic daddy-stash with *Penthouse* and *Playboy* going back two decades. This is

California hardbodies in the open air, bright flash colours, nothing older than a year.

I know he has some kiddie stuff here, he has to. I scratch my way to the bottom of his mess, furious, hysterical. There's a tear in the orange lining of the case and I rip it wider thinking I've found his secret stash.

This must be his unpublished collection. Polaroids with me as a baby and Arthur over me, Arthur with his finger in me, Arthur licking me, Arthur with his cock in my mouth. The colours change so quickly in my head that relief over proof of my sanity is changing to anger as I take the photos into the next room.

Arthur seems jolted seeing the pictures in my hands but he quickly buries the surprise. He's the victim of all this. He wants to know where I found the dirty pictures. Pictures of that young man and that dirty girl. Where did I get those?

I'm standing over him screaming that he's the young man and I'm the dirty girl. He's the dirty man and I'm the young girl. I'm pointing out these two people in the photograph in case he doesn't get it and then there's this tug on my hair. Cal's behind me and pulling my hair until I'm crying with the sudden knowledge of who took the pictures.

There is no one who will help me. There are the two men who pushed me in, standing at the edge of my sinkhole, but they just watch. There's a limit to how long I can hold my head above the muck.

Back out, leave, run from this place. They laugh now and will laugh forever. If mother were alive she would be on my side, protecting me. She must not have known. She knew nothing of what went on because she loved me and would have died for me and that's the truth because I said it.

Karen's mother ends up being the one I tell, not Karen herself because she wouldn't be able to take it in, but her mother because she is solid and can hear this. Tuesday, I tell her, when I know Karen and Roger have gone to a movie. It's raining and it takes about an hour to get it out. If she had been impatient I wouldn't have told her but she keeps pouring cup after cup of tea and makes that the whole focus of the hour, as if it is very important work, which it turns out to be.

When I'm done she holds me and feeds me those stupid, cliché, comforting lines that seem so impotent but actually work, like spells that aren't much to hear but do their magic anyway.

A week later I'm returning to my family of origin. The key still works in the lock. I suppose that means he's not afraid of me, but why would he be?

This is the way he used to approach me in my bedroom, quietly at night, a concerned parent checking on the child. Here I am at last, with freedom and power. I am conscious. He is not. But even as I fantasize a knife near his throat or a pillow over his face, I know I won't do it.

Back in the living room, I look around at the things I have given him to make him comfortable. The rice cooker for his birthday, the fountain pen set, the cordless phone, all gifts from the dutiful daughter, scattered with no particular care.

there is no mercy

Only the VCR seems to have attracted some pride of ownership and that is why I unplug the cables and pull it off the shelf, begin my final evacuation. I imagine the old man looking around his living room, wondering why he has so many video tapes, the problem briefly wrinkling his forehead, then fading.

Glue

I'M SURPRISED WHEN SEAN, WHO MAY OR MAY NOT BE MY SON, heaves himself up out of the water. Thousands of laps have made a muscular youth, nothing like the boy I remember. The coach talks to him for a few minutes before sending him to the change room. I watch for the moment when Sean will recognize me. He looks up but contains his expression. That's the way he's going to be now, very cool, not excited by anything.

The pizza is stringy and the Parmesan tastes funny but at least the waitress is giving us some space. I am annoyed at myself for coming to this conversation with strategy and tactics because he is not the enemy. Boxing him is harder than it used to be. He scans the waitresses while I talk and while I guess that's a good sign, it's still distracting.

—She just doesn't want you coming around any more. Or phoning.

—Do you like it when I come to visit? Should I stop coming to visit?

—She thinks I'm at the age where I need a positive role model.

—'Cause you wouldn't want to end up like me, living *my* horrible life.

—Yeah, I wouldn't want to end up like you.

—I haven't actually ended up yet.

The waitress has her timing down, appearing when Sean has just stuffed his face and I'm trying to say something important. Sean completely ignores her when she asks if everything is okay. I nod, she walks away, Sean stares at her ass.

—Why should I listen to you at all?

—I can teach you things.

—How to beat people up? How to rob them?

—Listen, if you're going to be like that, I'm not going to continue.

—No, don't let me stop you. They don't teach that stuff in school.

—That's right. They don't teach that kind of stuff in school. Some day you might get into real trouble and then you won't know what to do or say and it might turn out fine for you and it might not. And it pisses me off that you don't care because no one ever told me anything.

We eat pizza with our hands, like normal people, unlike Lisa who, if she were here, would be using a knife and fork to keep her fingers from getting greasy. We hold our greasy hands the same way, curled in, with the fingers fanning out. This is the best evidence so far that he is my son and not the product of one of his mother's interim fuck toys. Sean seems unconvinced.

—It could be socialization.

—What?

—It could just be the result of me being around you or someone else.

This exasperates me but I am secretly hopeful.

Any normal kid would just be happy to have skis like that but Sean wants to see the credit card, right there in Metrotown in front of Planet Superstar with shoppers flowing around us, a few of them taking notice.

There's a couple of rental cops heading this way and as Sean considers turning me in, I watch everything play on his face: first anger, then fear, then guilt. I could teach him how to keep his feelings off his face—that's one thing he could learn from me. He is angry at me again, because I appear to be relaxed, because I am relaxed, because I appear to know his thoughts, because I do know his thoughts, and he's going to let the guards pass, and he does.

Between the neighbours' fence and the tool shed I watch her as she moves to the phone. It's early Saturday, the grass needs cutting, my shoes are wet from the dew. She hangs up when she hears my voice and goes back to cleaning crumbs from the toaster, banging it over the sink as I have asked her many times not to do. The sink is not a garburator.

I want to climb this fence and stand in her backyard, facing her in my dark clothing. She lets it ring the second time, angering me. She should know that I am close enough to throw a brick through her window. I could cut the power to her house, turn off the gas, cut the phone line. I want her to see me as a wild fire. I want to frighten her, make her run at the sight of me. I will do it. I will enter her life.

Lisa's failure to understand my feelings must stem from a lack of imagination. If she relates to metaphors, I think that being locked out of her own house might make it clear.

I'm in the middle of changing the locks when Lisa's

neighbour drops by. And I don't mean straining to look over his fence, I mean right behind me, watching me work. I already hate the guy so much that I want to take a ball-peen hammer to his face. What arrogance. But I talk to him instead. Jarhead. Weaselly geek. If there were more at stake here I would make special plans for him. It's hard enough to work a deadbolt without having this guy behind me. He wonders if Lisa is home and there's a prick of panic, followed by a full second of anger that I panicked, but I get it back, start talking, feeling cocky, knowing that I'm going to ride over this guy. Oh, he doesn't want to disturb me, it's just that there have been a couple of break-ins in the area, that's all. Someone had backed up a truck to the Brisbanes' and had taken a whole bunch of their stuff in broad daylight. Oh, is that right, you fat fucking piece of shit.

I tell him about the strange calls that Lisa is getting. Harassment. She doesn't feel safe any more and suspects that she is being watched or stalked. He's hesitant but I know he'll eat this because he's weak and I'm rolling over him with confidence. As I finally get the deadbolt off, he's really starting to annoy me. I have to agree that people are just different these days, the streets aren't safe, we have to watch out for each other, etcetera, before he starts walking back to his house.

He's almost off the property when he turns sideways and looks at my car and I'm thinking, fuck, you fucking prick. I'm wearing work clothes but there's nothing in my car that makes me look like a locksmith, there's no company name, I don't have tools lying around. And it should be a van, not a car. He's looking at it, inside, the nosey prick, and then he goes back to the house. I have at least five minutes of work left and I don't know if he's going to call, or what the response time is here, or if the response would be silent, or what. Fuck him. I keep working and listening for anything, the speed of every car that approaches. No one is going to take me down like this. That is not going to happen.

I slip the lock on the patio door. I guess this means I'm still bitter. I thought I might be flooded with love and peace by the time I reached her house, maybe some remorse about the lock stunt, but that hasn't happened.

Maybe I'm too quick to give up on conventional means of persuasion. Maybe I should stop marrying women who are as stubborn as I am. Maybe I should have known her resolve when I saw Sean being escorted to the bus by the school security guard. Maybe I should read the papers more often so that I would know that schools have security guards now. Maybe I should stop passing on lucrative jobs just to muddle around in doomed personal projects. Maybe I should do my thing and get out of this house.

The thing about glue is that it's quiet. I have ten tubes of super-strong glue and the best hours of the morning. I do all the cupboards and drawers, the faucets, toilet handle, fridge door, stove knobs, telephone to cradle, dirty plates to counter top, kitchen chairs to floor. A little goes along the back of a tape before I put it in the VCR and press *play*. There's the remote, disk drive, keyboard, light switches, and by the time I'm finished, I'm having so much fun that I want to do the neighbours' as well.

You are as important as your hotel room, and tonight that is cause for depression. I don't walk from the bed to the bathroom, I make the journey. It might take an hour or six because I start by lying on the edge of the bed on my stomach with one arm hanging over the edge. I move closer to the edge until the bed cover loses its grip on my limp body. After I fall to the floor, I examine the stains from wine and coffee, a cigarette burn near the edge of the bed, imagine the hand it slipped from. My face is on this carpet. I trace the vague pathways of ten thousand smelly feet and wonder why I'm not repulsed.

The floor is rock bottom. I'd gladly sink further into dark oblivion, but the earth rejects me, leaving me flat on the surface.

I see wear patterns and compression, trails from the bed to the bathroom, a crooked door, scuff marks along the baseboards. Perhaps a small piece of nacho chip under the bed. I think that's what it is.

When you're on the floor you wonder why you ever wanted to be anywhere else. You wonder what you were thinking when your head was so much higher, closer to the ceiling, why activity made sense then but not now.

Finger. Light. Bed. Floor. Nouns without verbs or objects. Language without regulation quickly escapes meaning until you are lying on the floor of a hotel room wishing you were a noun. Everything else in the room seems smug in its identity, but the only thinking object here is in trouble.

Beyond my body, this room, beyond this room I can imagine the roof of this hotel. There is probably water pooling from this last week of rain. From the roof you would be able to see over Kingsway, perhaps as far as the mountains. Rising up slowly a few hundred metres, you would come through the clouds and be able to see one quarter of the moon and maybe Venus. This is not helpful.

I am ironing a shirt when Sean arrives. He props his bike up against the spare bed, turns on the TV and studies the shopping channel with desperate concentration, holding the clicker with both hands.

—She invited another role model over for dinner. As soon as he saw me I knew she hadn't told him about me. He brought over some expensive wine but she wouldn't let him drink it in front of me. He looked pissed off. The rest of the dinner he said mean things about her and about the house and after dinner they had this big fight when they thought I was upstairs. Then he left.

—He hates kids and treats women badly. That's some role model you have there.

Outside, someone is yelling about something small or something that will change their lives. The room is getting smaller. Every hour or so the walls move in a bit and I can't help but notice that everything in this room is an imitation of something of higher quality. Even the occupant.

—Do you have a girlfriend, Sean?

—Several.

—Tell me about them.

—No.

—Why not?

—Because I don't trust you.

—You keep cutting me down. Every time I see you it gets worse. You pass on everything that I offer and I want this to stop. There are things I want to teach you, things I want you to know about me.

—Okay, if you're so desperate to teach me something, then teach me something.

There's that anger again and I have to freeze my body to prevent myself from slapping him. I consider asking him to leave. I decide to have him iron my shirts instead.

Soon he knows that if it's a dark cotton, you have to turn it inside out to avoid the shine. That also makes it easier to work with the seams.

Spreading the shirt properly is important. Only patient people flatten it gently with their hands to check for bunches and folds. It's best to nose the iron between the buttons instead of cheating by gliding over them.

The free hand must always be active, guiding the movements of the iron, preparing a smooth flat surface. You must be perceptive and know the fabric, how it holds together. With a gentle pull, the wrinkles disappear.

After three shirts we've covered advance preparation, patience, negotiation and efficiency, the fine art of coaxing and its superiority over force. I know he's going to watch his mother the next time she irons something and he'll know that part of her as I do.

Sean has to go help his mother pack. She got a job somewhere back east. They leave on Saturday. That's all Sean is allowed to say. I don't press him as he puts on his coat and sits on the bed, staring at the wall. Finally he grabs the hotel stationery and writes out the address.

—Sorry about your house.

—What?

—Haven't you been home yet?

—No.

—I did some things to your house. Sorry.

He rides off before I can explain that it's nothing serious. I yell at him to come back but he ignores me. He'll be mad for a couple of hours or days or months and then we will be friends again. I've risked a lot these past days, for little gain, lost a war to a woman who can't even iron properly, but what can you say? Sometimes reason just loses.

Leila's Suburban Grass

ANDREW[1] BRAKES LIKE SOMEONE FROM TORONTO: RESENTFULLY and at the last second. It's a Mercedes though, and I've seen strangely reassuring ads of this car being crushed in a way that protects the occupants. Maybe it's the 100K force field, the aura of wealth that keeps us safe. Even a brick wall wouldn't let itself scratch a car like this.

---

1 Andrew
Age: 34
Morph Type: meso
Distinguishing Marks: Oddly healed metatarsal on right hand
Predicted Preferred Position: Scissor Legs

Review:
I am not impressed when that is someone's intention. It's hard to force a laugh when someone is telling another hilarious joke. They say that the quiet ones often lead secretly wild lives full of passion and recklessness. Often the quiet ones are just quiet and dull.

At dinner, it took half an hour for Andrew to exhaust his short list of things with which to impress a girl. We were on the second course with six to go and there was only so much you could say about the paintings on the ceiling. We both grew self-conscious when approached by grinning violinists.

I'm beginning to regret the punishing dating schedule I've arranged with select members of my investment club. The plan is to find a guy who gets me. This has emerged as my minimum requirement. I'm starting with the club members because despite a shared obsession with all things financial and an unashamed urge to declare net worth, they know me and they're easy targets. Like many of my projects, I'm having problems with the follow-through.

My hot feet are trapped in tortuous yet fashionable shoes, the kind designers love to inflict on women. Under my shoes there is carpet, metal, and eventually the violent scrape of asphalt under the car. The situation needs correction.

Quality of life is determined by what is beneath your feet. If you stand and look down right now, you will probably find carpet, tile, concrete or hardwood. This will not make your feet happy and since your feet are the communication link between you and the earth, the rest of you will not be happy either.

Foot-friendly surfaces include sand, water, air, dirt, rock, bark and grass. Sand that can be found on the beach along Olas Altas in Mazatlán. Water much like the water found in a pool, but preferably the calm water of Star Lake on Sunday morning when everyone is still sleeping off hangovers and the depth of the spot where you are swimming is unknown. Coastal air that rushes between your open toes as you sit on the branch of a tree down by the sea wall in Stanley Park. Dirt your feet might sink into if you were hoeing beets near Kleefeld. Rock similar to a bald-faced patch of Canadian Shield near Falcon Lake. Bark of a giant rotting tree that fell over twenty years ago in Cathedral Grove. And then there's grass.

I love suburban grass and all things connected to it: orange basketball hoops that are never used, silly globe-shaped BBQs that rust badly, any kind of sprinkler but especially the ones that fan back and forth or the ones that spray a slow arc, making that phut-ta phut-ta phut-ta sound.

I have body memories of grass, what it's like to walk on and the stains it gives to the soles of my feet and my knees. Somewhere in my brain lies the smell of it, freshly cut on a Saturday morning. If someone doesn't get that then they don't get me.

We speed toward Richmond, over the Oak Street Bridge, and all the losers in our way had better realize that and scuttle over to the right-hand lane. We pass them in every way— faster, richer and definitely better looking.

I slept on the couch at Andrew's apartment in Kits last night and now he thinks I've earned the right to his secrets. No one even knew he had a house. Whenever it was his turn, the group met at his apartment on Larch Street, marvelling at his TSE terminal and the "disciplined" (barren) accommodations. It's so Zen, as William[2] would say, sitting on the floor as we discussed junior mining stocks. There was nothing on the walls but paint. The regular stuff that might have left a hint of domestic warmth was all crammed into the second bedroom.

---

2 William
Age: 40
Morph Type: ecto
Predicted Distinguishing Marks: Webbed feet
Predicted Preferred Position: Baptist

Review:

William's house was a museum. There were no red velvet ropes, no glass boxes, just the curator running toward me, the ignorant gawker, as I bent over to sit down in his rocker. He scooped me up and guided me to the less valuable couch. I didn't listen to anything after 18th century, just kept nodding as he became calm and explained in plain and emphatic tones that I had almost seated myself in a display chair.

After I had examined one of his *très gauche* but apparently expensive figurines, he turned it a smidge to the left and rubbed off the finger acid with a soft cloth. He needed help that I didn't have the training to give him.

Last straw: I fetched a bottle from the cellar at his request and opened it without showing him my choice. I chose well, I think, judging from the way his face went red and purply veins started to throb near his temple as his fingers traced over the label. I might as well have handed him his first-born's heart on a china platter. I left him to grieve.

Andrew's telling me about the past five years while I try to think of an easy way to slip him Mark's[3] work number but I'm not sure Andrew or anyone else in the group knows Mark is a therapist. Andrew had a wife he'd never mentioned at our meetings. Susan's the one who insisted on the house.

He became suspicious of her a year into the marriage when she began disappearing in the evenings for appointments that she would not explain. He snooped a look at her appointment book, which had the letter H written in, the same time each week. After a year and a half of suspecting but not confronting her, he decided to rent an apartment in Kitsilano in order to have an affair of his own. Every night that Susan had an H in her book, he went out to Yaletown

---

3 Mark
Age: 47
Morph Type: endo
Distinguishing Marks: Scars from numerous beatings
Preferred Position: Doggy

Review:
    Sometimes a therapist will latch on to some small thing you've said and try to wrap a theory around it. At a certain point, the therapist must continue with his or her idea because to abandon it would make them look foolish, their techniques, random. Mark isn't like that.
    We've been all over the place, using all kinds of different models to understand my situation. He says there have been as many surprises for him as for me. Mark wants me to explore my feelings about grass. For six months we've been discussing grass and I have this fear now of exploding in laughter at the moment when I won't be able to be bizarre yet straight, like a comedian who can't stop himself from laughing at his own joke.
    Sometimes a therapist will fall in love with you, even as he explains how wrong that is. You will wonder what excites him more—the sudden affection for a client or the violation of his professional ethics. He will mention many times over dinner that the proper thing to do is to terminate the relationship but he will never get around to it. And as you sit in his BMW, outside your place, waiting for him to kiss you, you will be excited too, by the power you have to compromise him in this way, to break down his virtue with the power of attraction.

in his flash clothes with two thousand dollars in his pocket. He never spent much of it, but every time he brought out his wad to pay for a drink, people seemed astounded. It was a nerdish but surprisingly effective way of attracting the gullible and the greedy.

These joinings never lasted long, usually ending when she figured out that he wouldn't take her shopping, buy her nice things or go dancing every night. And when they left, some of them would say horribly personal things about his penis or his technique.

His true objective was to be discovered by Susan. He dropped little slips of paper with names and numbers, dabbed perfume on his collar from a bottle he kept in the glove compartment, and spread long hairs around his home like tinsel.

He didn't notice Susan setting up her own clues. At first, fifty dollars worth of 6/49 Quickpicks that she put up on the fridge. Then old Scratch and Lose tickets in the cracks between the couch cushions and under the stacks of annual reports he kept on his desk. When he finally asked her about the tickets they had a huge fight that revealed Susan's gambling addiction (H meant Hastings Park Racecourse, not Harold). Andrew struggled to explain the affairs he had had to punish her for the affair she had never had. He had a difficult time thinking of a precedent for this situation that could guide his actions. He moved his essentials out of the house and into the apartment that night.

Andrew and Gregor[4] prove that the best way to attract secrets is to be indifferent to them. Gregor phoned last Friday at 3:10 AM because he had used extreme methods to peek at an assay from Tavarex and wanted moral approval before trading on it. I made noncommittal noises but bought 100,000 shares on Monday morning.

I yank the wheel to the right, forcing Andrew to turn into the Dairy Queen parking lot. It's probably been twenty years since he last came here and now, a dilemma: stay near the car and risk being seen from the road or actually risk being seen inside. I watch him from the counter as he leans against the trunk of his car, using his hand to shield his face.

Back on the road, I force-feed ice-cream, which he seems to enjoy, making weak protests while I smudge his chin

---

4 Gregor
Age: 31
Morph Type: meso
Distinguishing Marks: Missing extreme tip of ring finger
Preferred Position: The Limbaugh

Review:

Two hours into the limo ride to Whistler and I had heard most of the Gregor Clark story, not the entire saga, but the parts he hoped would impress. I didn't care that he bought Newbridge at the bottom. Lunch with Anthony Robbins was something only one of them would remember.

He asked me to sing. He hadn't been talking about singing, this just came from nowhere. I told him that most performers were reluctant to sing in moving vehicles because of the inability to control minute movements of the diaphragm and he believed me. It was the only point in the evening when he looked interested in me and the sudden attention was uncomfortable. Luckily, a few minutes later, he resumed his monologue.

To summarize our date, there was no grass at Whistler, there was no grass on the Pacific Ocean, there was no grass at the Ford Centre or in his Lotus and there was no grass in his apartment, although I might have spotted some with the impressively phallic telescope he kept on the balcony. It was a penthouse, of course, close to Robson but far above all the earth-hugging vermin. Everything was very clean and very expensive and I did not like it.

white. His smile fades as we pull up to a red light across from two giggling Chinese girls in a z3 Roadster. I can see the jaw muscles near his ear tensing as we squeal off the line. There's a temper in there somewhere, as is often the case with smooth, clean men.

Taking me to Minivan Central is like telling me a horrible secret and I understand that. I mean, this far out of Kits and I feel like I'm in *Heart of Darkness*.

The house is a disappointment. It's trickery in a way—you see his car and you expect an equally extravagant house but it's clustered right in with the other ones, desperately trying to avoid a personality. And the grass in front, what little there is, unloved and sterile. Susan's gone, the house she once loved ruined by bad associations.

I hope the secrets will keep coming, that Andrew will unravel into something better or more like something I want. There is no time for me to be depressed as Andrew explains to me that this is not his taste, pushing me from behind, through the foyer with its pretty drop mats, past the living room full of overstuffed Sears-type furniture, down the hallway, past inoffensive and meaningless framed watercolours and into the back, an expanse of green that nearly knocks the wind out of me.

It goes deep, almost 150 feet to the back fence and almost as wide. Primped, preened, aerated, healthy, cooling blades of Kentucky bluegrass welcome my liberated feet. I throw my shoes to the side and lie down to study vapour trails, scan the clouds for patterns. I am dressed for concrete but grass forgives, stains me, welcomes me back.

Once I tried to explain grass and the inner child to Tony,[5] babbling on about how our distance from grass increased as we aged, but he just looked at me as if I were insane. From the moment we put on shoes we are engaged in a weaning process that leads to permanent separation from the surface of the earth, decisions being made in glass towers and steel bunkers. Without grass, without earth contact, there is no point of reference to balance out abstraction. I have $472,000 and every day I try to decide if that makes me rich. There's a lot of paper in my study, but otherwise you wouldn't know. I'm not a lifestyle rich person. I don't feel the money.

Andrew is cunning or lucky, taking me to this place of worship where the grass isn't grey from exhaust or full of goose turds, beer caps and condoms. It hasn't been used as trim by some architect or perfected to speed the roll of a ball. This grass invites lemonade and popsicles and the occasional bee sting. People set

---

5 Tony
Age: 41
Morph Type: ecto
Distinguishing Marks: Slightly off-centre nose
Preferred Position: Female Dominate

Review:
After Gregor I decided to cancel the rest of the dates but Tony wouldn't let me. Poor Tony, all his efforts and desire, not at all interesting or unique. Sleep, I wanted sleep, but he wouldn't stop playing piano, after I had already wormed my way under his duvet. He wanted me to sing. He had asked earlier in the evening and I had refused. I was getting nervous about these repeated requests for my voice. No one would or could explain what was going on.

The smoky jazz club, that was fine, I had no problem with that, I like fine music, but that doesn't make me want to sing along. I don't know what he was expecting, that given the proper environment, I would get up on our table and start, a spotlight from the back swinging over to me, the band waiting for my cue. Now I'd have to say I prefer any indifferent room to the claustrophobia of intense desire.

Tony came pretty close, but in the end I resented it. He was a wonderful pianist but it was three in the morning and I did say I was tired and going to bed and he did take in that information and he did ignore it. After half an hour or so I came out to the living room and he seemed less surprised than I thought to see me naked. He didn't stop playing as I came up behind him and undid his belt. Within a few minutes he had to push the bench back to give me room and that was it for the piano playing.

up wading pools and swing sets on grass like this. I never thought Andrew would be the one to find my aesthetic G-spot.

From the house he brings a giant glass pitcher of lemonade and stands over me like a waiter or a servant. He won't sit down because the grass might stain his pants. His head partially blocks the sun and he seems to enjoy torturing my retinas by alternately giving them shade, then blinding them.

The tactile makes the abstract irrelevant. We think with our minds but we live with our bodies. Andrew repeats these words back to me, assuring me that he knew what I meant. He thinks it explains my tendency to go barefoot at meetings, the time I insisted on feeling Gregor's thick silk shirt, how I touch almost anything that attracts me. I vaguely remember saying something like that after a meeting, during some bizarre tangential debate with Tony, who waited two beats and then continued on to something else like an impatient reader skipping over an unknown word.

Andrew says that for him it's fishing, which is just as rich in sensation despite its redneck, Canadian Tire, family values, Norman Rockwell connotations. You can own a lake if you get up early enough, while the mist is still rising. In a fibreglass canoe the only sounds are water dribbling off the end of your paddle as you raise it from the water and gurgling eddies from your stroke. There is no way to describe the feel of the rod when something live takes your hook.

I ask him why he is the only one who hasn't asked me to sing. At our club meeting about a month ago, I had sung a few lines from an Ella Fitzgerald song to settle a disagreement, and since then almost every one of the guys from the club I've dated has pressed me to sing in private, as if it's important, as if talent is an endangered species.

I have a good voice. I have an excellent voice but I don't want to be a singer because it's a shitty life. I write songs, though, and some have done well, but I don't sing around other people because if I do people think I should be happy to do it anytime, on demand, and wouldn't if be great if I would sing at so-and-so's wedding or what's-her-face's funeral, this-or-that charity event.

The rigidity in Andrew's body seems to leave as he lies down on the grass beside me with his head propped up on one hand. He has been tempted to ask for a long time. He thinks I'm naïve for letting loose like that and expecting everything to be the same. If a woman has a great voice, singing can do dangerous things to the lust levels of the average man. He wants a private show like the rest of them but thinks it would be a weird thing to ask of me—too personal, too intimate.

Andrew takes my hand and leads me to the garden shed, and the smell when he yanks that creaky aluminum door open shoots me back a few decades into dust, humidity and grass clippings. He's breathing it in too, knows the value of it and we stand there in the doorway until I pull him close and sing quietly into his ear a song I've been working on, not quite finished.

I kiss his small sunburnt ear. His eyes are closed as he leans against the door of the shed. It's a long time before he tells me he wants to know the feel of me.

Up in the bedroom I make him guess what each part of me would feel like before I let him find out for sure. His hand grazing the tiny blond hairs on my forearm. The small of my back, the feel of fabric pulled over my skin. His hands resting on my hips. His hands through my hair. My chest against his chest, against his face. His leg edging my legs apart. The delicate point of his tongue parting my lips. Can he guess where the thigh turns into upper thigh? Can he find that spot?

He trembles with anticipation.

Andrew moves with new grace. Andrew, no relation to the Andrew of our first doomed date, brings me back down to the garden shed for my promised surprise. He shows me his tiny museum of webbing-style lawn chairs, ancient garden tools, musty ball gloves, and in the corner, underneath the clipping bag, lawn darts, the holiest of holy outdoor games.

It takes quite a throw to reach the hoop. Andrew looks like he might pull something at first but he improves quickly. I fluke out, arc one high, right into the hoop. It makes me think of all the kiddies who had their eyes poked out before this game was banned. When we played this as kids sometimes one of us would throw the dart straight up by accident and no one could see where it went because of the sun and everyone would scream and cover their heads and wait for that dart to come down, wait forever under the hot sun.

Elegy

9:30 AM, Pontiac Grand Am, Eastbound

Adam passes Kari as he checks for an opportunity to pass the green pickup that has been holding him up since Churney Road. The driver might be drunk, judging from how he drifts between the centre line and the gravel shoulder, rocks in the wheel wells warning from the right, car horns warning from the left.

Adam is the science teacher at Carlyle High who took Kari aside and tried as vaguely and casually as possible to draw attention to the red spot forming at the crotch of her white jeans. She assumed he wanted to talk about the D- on her latest test, following a string of As. He thought of how you usually alert others by touching the same part on your own body. He wasn't about to touch his own crotch. And staring at her crotch also seemed like a bad idea.

He asked her if she had been to the washroom recently and she looked at him, stunned. When he said, you're bleeding, she touched under her nose. He had to clarify by saying, you're bleeding down there. She gasped and backed away from him, covering the red spot with a textbook. They were both sorry that it hadn't been a female teacher who had pointed this out.

Kari's body looks like trash. It's dead meat but not the wrapped-in-plastic kind you might pick up in the store, not even the kind that lies in the basement of some scientific institution, in cold storage, ready to be useful. Her meat is trash, something once useful but now discarded. The tuft of hair that isn't matted down blows in the wind like the fur on a road-kill rabbit.

9:34 AM, Chevy Cavalier, Westbound

Bill is fighting with Evelyn again about the restaurant. The meat supplier seems to be packing the patties with too much ice, ripping him off, and Evelyn wants him to switch suppliers but he can't be bothered. They always screw the little guy no matter where you go.

Bill's so tired of her talking about it that he considers slamming the breaks while she puts on her makeup, just to change the subject. He lets out a giant sigh just as they pass the body formerly known as Kari.

Bill knew Kari as the quiet one of that rowdy after-school crowd, the one who made her fries soggy with vinegar and never failed to say thank you, almost formally, whenever she picked up her order.

9:47 AM, Ford F-150, Eastbound

Vance guides his grunting shit wagon onto the road, missing the shift into third, grinding, missing it again, grinding, missing again before using both hands to ram it in, up and to the right.

He snorts up a big gob of phlegm and horks it out the window. It lands on some gravel, about ninety feet away from

Kari. Three weeks before she was killed she saw him do this as he came out of the hardware store: he horked out some nasty horrible clump of himself and she was repulsed, making a big show about stepping around it for the benefit of her friends. He didn't notice.

In total he's had three encounters with her: honking at her as she walked home from a party, ogling her breasts while she tanned in the park with her girlfriends, and seeing her sing in the choir at the Christmas concert last year. He's more likely to remember her breasts or her ass than her face.

If Vance knew that Kari was beginning to rot just across the ditch on the ridge where the trees started he would place her in his mind before she was killed, doing something dangerous with a dangerous man, an out-of-towner, because this would help him make sense of it. Bad things happened when you wandered off, drunk or stoned, separated from the pack. A girl shouldn't tease a guy and then get all uppity when he wants some. What did she expect? What was she thinking?

9:53 AM, Dodge Charger, Westbound

Dana stubs out a cigarette as she flies by the murder site at 120K. She makes it roar at 6000 RPM before sticking it in fourth and Randy's words come back to her like Obi-wan fuckin' Kenobi: it's a rocket, not a cruiser. It's good off the line but don't run it fast down the highway. Randy assumed that Dana drove his car nice, like his other girlfriends had, but people across town could hear how Dana drove Randy's car and it was not nice.

Randy's friend Duncan once borrowed Randy's car to take Kari on a date. Kari and Duncan didn't have much to say to each other and when he started talking about the car, hoping to impress, she glazed over. To her it was a car like any other. It had doors and wheels and seats and it generally moved forward.

He explained the function of the scoop at the front, the fat tires at the back and the carburetor that was as big as a toilet bowl. He did not get lucky with her that night. In fact, it would be a year and a half before he lost his virginity.

10:01 AM, Oldsmobile Cutlass, Eastbound

Kenneth cruises along in his Cutlass while eating a piece of cold pizza from the night before and burning his tongue on coffee. The pizza comes from Danny's Pizza Shack and the excess sauce makes the congealed cheese mass slide off the slice and Kenneth says, shit.

Whenever Kari went to the Pizza Shack she loaded up her Greek special with Parmesan cheese and pepper flakes because they were free. It didn't seem to matter that it obscured the true taste of the pizza. It was extra value. She would ask for a sharp knife if one were not provided because she hated sawing away at the crust with a butter knife. That seemed like a waste of her time.

The Pizza Shack was also where Alex McFerron had felt her knee after the skating party while he was talking to the girl on his other side. For weeks Kari waited for him to make a legit-imate advance but he never did. A month later he was dating Monica Vernoff and Kari was angry at herself for wasting time on that loser, for positioning herself in the halls, timing her arrival at her locker with his, waiting by the phone for entire evenings.

10:11 AM, Toyota Corolla, Westbound

Warren's late again, speeding towards a store that should be open by now. Late or lucky—it really depends on when the boss gets there. Being ahead of it, he doesn't notice the blue cloud that comes out of his rust bucket Toyota and drifts across the road and into the trees, a blue horrid smoke that would have made Kari cough and maybe pinch her nostrils together to protect her perfectly pink lungs.

All the holes in her body are now open and close to the ground. A small bird picks a bug from her labia, ripping out a single curly hair in the process. A beetle knocks its feelers against a clot of dried semen near her belly button. The sun warms and dries the skin on the right side of her body.

10:15 AM, Ford Aerostar, Eastbound

If I looked like you I'd feel like a goddess. Cheryl didn't know that Kari had once said that to Cheryl's daughter, Veronica. Cheryl was as oblivious to the intimate connection the two girls had as to the squirrel that runs across the road in front of her van. She misses a lot of things but if you showed her a picture of Kari she'd probably recognize her as the creepy kid who spent way too much time with her lovely daughter. She didn't pass on Kari's messages. She hated Kari's mother, a woman who shopped in sweat pants and smelled funny: a faint mix of piss and cigarettes. It was best to limit Veronica's exposure to those types.

Veronica rescued Kari in seventh grade, dragging her up from terminal loser status to a level of acceptance and respect. She couldn't manage to push Kari over into the cool zone. There were limits to her social power and her friend didn't take hints on the clothes and the hair. Kari was always there and the people who liked Veronica learned to accept her. The two girls became a package deal. Some thought they might be lesbians but this was said more as a joke because no one actually believed there could be lesbians in their town.

10:23 AM, Buick Skylark, Eastbound

Gladys is a bad driver. She doesn't know it but the three drivers behind her do. She brakes when she has the right of way and barrels through when it's imperative that she stop. Other cars are distracting to her and other drivers seem almost violent in their actions. She wishes she had the road to herself.

She changes to the golden oldies station and passes Kari on her right. Gladys knows more than she'd like to about Kari, Sharon's troublesome daughter. She knows that Kari was a difficult labour, a difficult child, and a difficult teenager.

Kari had a habit of creating art projects all over the house. Just recently she made a little man with dinner forks and a soldering iron. Sharon tried to explain that the house and its contents were not raw material for artistic expression. Kari had no concept of the proper place for things. As Sharon had often explained, pictures were for walls and photo albums, paintings were for rich people and art galleries, and sculpture belonged on the lawns of public buildings in the city.

She did her best to scrub off pictures drawn in felt marker that appeared under the dining room table, at the bottom of a bathroom drawer, under the stairs or on the side of the washing machine.

Sometimes Gladys faded out during those long whiny conversations. Her input wasn't really required anyway. She threw in the occasional uh-huh and is-that-right while she watched the muted TV.

10:25 AM, Dodge Ram, Westbound

Dan passes Kari just as he checks on the load of paint cans in the back of his truck. He plans to do the hand railings around the school even though he knows that the skate punks will strip the tops clean in a few months.

He's friendly with the kids who hang around after school and sometimes he lets them in while he cleans. It's a slack job at night and he prefers talking to the kids to scrubbing toilets.

Dan once saw Kari vandalizing the log swing in the playground. He yelled out and started running toward her and she took off across the field as if being pursued by a pack of dogs. When he got to the log he noticed the carving knife on the ground and the profile carved into the top of the log.

Dan didn't know much about art but the horse's head the kid had carved was impressive. It was so good he wanted to tell someone about it. He wanted her teachers to know she had talent. It seemed important. Later Dan's girlfriend pointed out that the principal probably wouldn't appreciate the artistic merit of vandalism on school grounds.

10:37 AM, Honda Civic, Eastbound

Michelle checks her sleeping child in the rearview mirror and smiles. An ant crawls into Kari's nostril as the car passes. The woman who occasionally babysits Michelle's baby is the sister of the man whose cousin runs the feedlot that employs David. David rents a room in the basement of the house owned by the man who gave Kari a ride last night.

Usually Kari did not take rides but it was raining and there was lightning and the strikes were getting closer as she got into his Plymouth Fury.

—You know, in Europe, if a guy gives a girl a ride, he usually gets a blow job out of it. That's what they do in Europe.

After a few minutes he asked her if she wanted to have sex but she didn't hear him over the radio. She was too busy whittling away at a cork with her jackknife, getting the shavings all over the seat.

—Hey, are you listening to me?

The tire tracks of the Fury stop thirty feet from Kari's body.

The muddy tracks show where the car slipped into a rut on that turnaround and he panicked, flooring it, packing great wads of mud into the wheel wells.

He wakes up in the morning having almost forgotten what happened until he sees the streaks of mud on the back fender. He'll go to another town to wash it off. From now on he'll keep the car really clean.

Kari's retinas face the northeast quarter of the sky. Today she has a view of the blue sky cut only by the phone lines that run along the road. At night, Cassiopeia, Triangulum, Andromeda, and Perseus will pass through her steady gaze.

What Other People Have

—HEY, RICHIE RICH, WHERE DO YOU GET YOUR MONEY?

—Richard works for his money. Have you heard of that?

She doesn't turn around to look at me in the backseat but I can tell that Clara's enraged by my shock-jock interview style. If it weren't for Richard's presence, we'd be fighting by now. When we were dating we weren't very good at fighting, despite all the practice. She would spray me with angry words and instead of listening I would notice the perfect fullness of her sweet-tasting lips, the extra colour that seemed to come to her eyes when she was mad. She would try very hard to hurt me, cycling through her list of swears until she was too tired to maintain her level of rage. My calm would wear her down.

Clara has become even more beautiful in the six months since she has replaced me with Richard. If she were not off-limits to me I would lean forward and kiss the tiny blonde hairs on the back of her neck.

Richard turns the stereo down and accelerates out of a curve, 150 now. He says that for six months he's been working full-time, partly because his friends tease him about the trust fund. He hasn't drawn on it since he started working. I lean forward again, close enough to bite his ear.

—What's your total annual income if you add the fund and your net pay?

The question is a rude one and Richard turns the volume back up in reply. I feel like a misbehaving child on a family outing as Clara, the scolding mother, turns in her seat to deliver the look that became common toward the end of our relationship: still mad about us, about everything. Her intent is to show anger but Clara's glare looks like a pose from a fashion magazine, some pouty model selling jeans.

I like Richard's Mercedes. Near 120 my Eagle Vista begins to shudder and rattle as if it's approaching the speed of sound. You start thinking about loosened bolts and the strength of welded joints. My car's an out-of-shape man, running and screaming. Rich's car is a sexy woman cooing, 180, 205, cruising now at 215, faster?

A year ago I took this route with Clara in the Vista. The front shocks needed replacing (still do), making the front end bounce like an amusement park ride, and all the way there I was harassed by assholes in low, shiny, tinted glass riding a few feet behind while I sped up to be accommodating, 80 sometimes 90 into the turns, the car shaking and beginning to stink.

Now I'm with the asshole, sliding back into the leather. The danger of cliffs diminishes slightly as we pass, ignoring signs meant for poor people in slow-moving cars.

—Is this restaurant like slumming for you, Richie Rich?

—Don't call me that, okay?

The big man orders wine without consulting us.

—How do you know we want that?

—Want what?

—The wine you ordered.

—Which was?

—What you just ordered.

—You've decided you don't like it but you can't name the wine. It's a good wine. It goes with what we're eating. If it offends your delicate buds we can order another.

Rich is an excellent playmate, his face an exhibition of winces, eye-rolls, aversions and blushes. Just now, a deflating sigh as I lick the shrimp sauce off my fingers, use bread to sop up what remains on the plate. When I'm into my second basket, the waiter comes by to suck up my pile of crumbs with a hand-held sweeper. Whoops, I drop my napkin on the floor, oh dear me, and once again before I wipe my mouth and why not my nose as well. Where are the entrées?

Rich tries to nudge us toward civility by expressing an interest.

—Clara tells me you're a painter?

—No.

Clara gives me a flat look as Rich carries on.

—I have a few pieces. I picked up something by Joe Average at the AIDS benefit last year.

—The big one? The 10K one?

—Yeah, the big one. You could come over and check it out if you want.

—Come to your place and prostrate myself in front of a *real* artist's work. Yeah. I'll do that.

I get the waiter to name the tiny pumpkins on my plate, then send it back to the kitchen for regular vegetables. He returns with broccoli, carrots and a black velvet box. Rich makes the cut throat sign until the waiter figures it out but I manage to snag his arm and make a grab for the box as he heads back to the kitchen. Rich blasts off his seat and lunges over the table for the box, spilling his wine.

His hand shakes from the adrenaline shot as he gives the reclaimed box to Clara. The necklace scores him a peck on the cheek before she leans over to show me. I reach out to touch it and Richie's half out of his chair again. My hands go up, arrest style, until he slowly settles back.

—I arranged this before I knew it'd be the three of us.

She starts to put it on but Rich explains that it's not an everyday use kind of necklace. It's more like a special event thing, not something you'd want to lose while romping around in a meadow or doing an aerobics class. For now it will be returned to the darkness of the restaurant safe.

Around the time that Clara's unfinished dessert comes back wrapped in tin foil shaped like a swan, I slap down my maxed-out Visa and tell them that I've got this one, hoping to provoke the usual fight over who pays. He says thanks and heads for the washroom. She smiles sweetly as I pressure her to cover me.

—Okay, very amusing. Now give me some money. You know I can't pay for this.

—What about this flash looking gold card? I'm very impressed.

—I'll pay you back.

—When?

—Next week?

—Which friend will you borrow from to repay me? I should do you a favour and cut this up. Maybe the waiter has a pair of scissors in the kitchen.

Straighter in her chair, she moves her wallet to the other side, out of my reach. Her eyes follow my hands. I talk until her spine relaxes and her arms come down. The shoulders must roll over, round and curved forward, an enclosing, accepting surrender. As I walk away she will switch the cards.

By the ticket booth they are an obvious couple and in a sur-prise attack of empathy, I want to allow them some time together. Instead of taking the ski-lift I could go on a nature walk or visit one of the alpine meadows but Clara grabs my jacket and pulls me in.

Four o'clock is late to be going up the mountain. Gondolas coming down the other side are full of people who've spent most of the afternoon up there. Each time we go over the rollers the car shudders, making the noise of a mechanized object out of control. The flimsy wire guards are almost as worrisome as the improvised angles of the beams supporting this whole unlikely structure.

The lovers relax into each other on the opposite side of the car until I spot a bear and two cubs running into the bush, just before the first station. Clara and Rich turn and stand in my way so I step onto the bench to look over them, crushing Rich's sunglasses.

—Sorry. I'll buy you a new pair.

—Like you bought me lunch?

—No, really, I'll pay for them. How much were they?

—Forget about it.

—Tell me. It can't be that much.

Rich keeps fidgeting with the mangled frames, examining them from many angles as if considering how to fix what is beyond the talents of any fixer.

—If it makes you feel any better you can stomp on my watch. Here. Go ahead. Stomp on it, Money Boy. Balance our accounts.

Clara laughs, then tries to stifle it. The creases above Rich's nose deepen as Clara runs out of air, and it makes me wonder what he had expected of an afternoon with someone he loves and the spoiler of everything. I say something stupid, she laughs at it and I laugh at her laughter. The people coming down stare at us, their idiotic gawking the funniest thing.

Richard stomps out past the observation deck and down the road as soon as the door opens, disappearing into the woods before we can catch up. Clara is far away but I can hear her jacket rustle when she turns around to look back at the lift station. I also hear the blood that moves through my brain as I stand like a charcoal smudge on clean canvas. I want to say something worthy of this place but ask for her glasses instead. I think it's cataracts you get from exposure at these elevations and probably cancer too. With no sun block I can almost feel my cells mutate. The glasses cut annoying lines in the panorama but help me scope the source of the noise: tourists on the observation deck shouting banalities back and forth, unaware that they are the only sound.

Clara climbs onto a bulldozer, shifting and jerking the levers so violently that I'm glad she hasn't found the ignition. She bends to listen to my confession.

—I want you very much, Clara. Right now.

—That doesn't surprise me.

—Because you feel the same way?

—No. Because you don't value love. You value what other people have.

She turns away to study the progress of a truck moving down the slope, a heavy load bucking and clattering in the back. Her neck is open and exposed. If I moved closer I could take in the scent of her shampoo, closer still, the discreet dab of Fendi on her neck.

—Why did you invite me here? It would have been more fun with just the two of you.

—I heard him on the phone once. He told his friend that he was totally overwhelmed by me. Ever felt that way about a girl?

With one hand on the cab support I swing down to kiss her just as she steps down to the tread with renewed interest in Richard's location.

Clara thinks we'd cover more ground if we split up. I mention that being together keeps the bears away now that the sun's going down and we're alone up here, alone except for the bears. She won't turn around for that, or for pleas, or for whining, or even very loud cursing.

A bear will pick up my scent and having seen the other bipeds move away, will begin to advance. It won't want the others because they've proven themselves healthy and fast, capable of fighting. The bear will come for me because I'm moping about in circles, obviously lame or old or not quite right in the head. Easy prey that's just as tasty, not tough, plenty of tender fatty tissue. He'll sniff me, growl, then rip my scrotum off, causing pulsing arcs of blood to splatter the snow.

The sun moves quickly toward the mountain ridge and glaring at it doesn't seem to slow it down. We are animals again, equalized, unless there's a Global Positioning System built into Richie's Movado, or his bulky jacket converts into a para-glider. Our bodies cool, our toes go numb at the same time. The bears won't care that I bought my shirt from Mark's Work Warehouse and Richie's came from Dunn's. It's just a wrapper to be ripped away. The staff won't come looking for us until the feeding frenzy has ended. The bears will fight over light meat or dark.

I'll be thinking of Clara when the bears get me. She was one of the few who didn't scrape me off at the first sign of trouble or harden against my pleas. I was out of money and places to stay when I met her. She let me sleep on her couch, just for the night, which turned into a week, a month. Later, a top-up on the Vista's insurance, just a couple hundred till the next pogey cheque came in, and soon after it's Xmas, is your heart made of stone, woman? I'll pay you back next week, I swear, again, just as soon as, that's a promise, here's an I.O.U.

But I was good to her, too, patient in those first few months of crying on my chest, crying because no one was forcing her to cheer up through cramps, trauma or a day at work that demanded total mental shut-down in front of the television.

She locked me out once, early on, pretended not to be home. My duffle bag out in the hall, next to the door, filled with my stuff, with a little note to explain things and smooth out my abrupt exit. Not strong enough to do this face to face, etc. I knocked once quietly then curled up on the floor against the far wall so she could see me from the peephole. Three times in two hours she checked on me and each time I heard the hardwood creak I closed my eyes. On the fourth visit the deadbolt cracked open.

It hits the back of my head and I brace against the bear, the avalanche...the snowball, its grainy ice working down the inside of my jacket, soaking my shirt.

Clara and Rich continue to pelt me but with the adrenaline I'm able to run down Rich and mash a handful of snow into his face. Clara, much farther ahead, screams when she checks my progress. I'm light, running after her, cursing her damn aerobics classes. I dive for her, hanging onto the bottom of her jacket until she falls.

Far away, a tiny man makes a tiny sound. The woman in my hands struggles and we slip down the bank until Rich, the bug man, has vanished. We lie quietly, keeping each other's limbs fixed in place. I should kiss her before the bug man returns to full size.

I'm relieved when Rich pulls over near Big Chief to get another look at the rock face. He doesn't drive much slower at night and I was having flashes of the car rolling, airbags exploding into me from every direction. There's not much to see in the dark but we go up onto the bluff and lie down on a blanket in the tall grass.

Halfway up the rock face a climber's light swings down, then up, as if the climber is searching for something. We might be looking at someone with a broken leg, twisting on his rope or someone who has lost a vital piece of equipment. Clara suggests that we stay silent to hear if the guy is screaming for help but one of us always breaks the silence within seconds.

If a jagged rock cut through that rope he would be living my recurring dream, falling toward the bottom, which, covered in shadows and darkness, cannot be seen.

I can still taste Clara's mountaintop kiss as I lie beside her. On her other side, Rich moves closer to her warmth than I am allowed. Soon we'll go back to the car, crisis or not, leaving the climber hanging and unaware of how beautiful it looks from here.

Standard Trip Planning for Christians

THE MIGHTY V-8 IN TIM'S SHAGGIN' WAGON FORCES ANOTHER gas stop. Shelby slips through the cabin curtains and by the time I join her she has already started, head tilted back, reaching for the packed groin of the gas boy in his blue coveralls on the other side of the dark tinted window. I unbutton my jeans while she begs in a whisper for the gas boy to pump until it bubbles and sloshes out of the tank. The smell of gas, a dirty perfume on meaty fingers that pull pipes apart, yank hoses off, screw on nuts without a wrench.

Later that day she leans over for the tenth time to check the gas gauge that still shows half full. She spots a rest area ahead and tugs on the wheel instead of asking me to pull over. When I slam the brakes to make the exit the van shudders and pulls to the left, our gear and other loose items crash into the back of my seat. Her urges, without external restrictions, have accelerated.

I pull in between two RVs while she puts the folding cardboard sun blocker up on the dash. The plan when we left Vancouver was six-hour breaks to create pent-up demand, but it isn't working. Every two hours now, even more often than usual. As punishment for pinching her abs, she spins around to put me in a headlock. I worm out of that and straddle her, pin her arms down until she bucks me off, head first into the wall, my forehead burned by the shag. I don't joke about her being stronger than I am anymore. My only defence against a four-day training split and protein shakes is to trick her into skipping as many workouts as possible.

She's on me again, before I can react. Extremities flushed with blood, cardio capacity near peak, she pulls my shirt off, runs her tongue up from my belly button.

After a seven with fifteen contractions, I pull on shorts and stumble out of the van, past the parking posts and onto the dry, prickly grass. Looking back I notice that the sun blocker on the windshield commands some good Samaritan to CALL POLICE.

Southern Alberta. The last time I visited the family home their answering machine had a message from a guy who requested ten prayers for a safe trip for the church youth group. Maybe he wanted one prayer from ten different people. He was very specific about the number. I wondered if five people at two prayers each would be okay. If only nine prayers came in, would God's protection be pro-rated? Were prayers on the caller's pre-trip checklist, just under mosquito repellant and emergency ass-wipe?

It's dark when we crunch onto the gravel, creeping into a nest of cars. My father's house seems unchanged on approach: the screen door still ripped at the bottom where the kids push on it, the same crusty work boots on last week's newspaper, the same caps hanging off the coat hooks. Everyone's at the table enjoying a late-night snack.

I apologize for missing the funeral, consider using the excuse of a crisis at work, but settle for the safer took-longer-than-expected line. Shelby, whose suit hangs useless from a coat hook in the van, gives me a fiery look.

After introductions, the new sinner stands with her arms crossed, her shoulders curved forward, finally taking a step back from the heat of all that attention. It looked fine on the road but here on the homestead her favourite aerobics top now looks—well, kind of slutty.

I tell them it's been a long, exhausting trip, put my arm around Shelby and plod upstairs in search of somewhere to crash. Dan's hand is on my shoulder before we reach the end of the hall. He offers his room to Shelby. I shrug off his grip, push Shelby over onto the bed and flop down beside her.

—Dad wouldn't permit it.

—He is dead, isn't he?

Lucy comes up a few minutes after Dan leaves. As always, her soothing tones follow his harsh words and I bend until I break. She sends us down from the usual sleeping place for good Christian folk, out the door, down the steps to the level of the earth, where the animals sleep, but righteous animals, Christian animals. There is an even lower place for us, a ditch perhaps, where we cannot contaminate the minds of children with dark oozing sin.

We'll sleep in the van again, only tonight we can use the side mirrors to watch the kitchen show, a discussion about doing the right thing. Not really much of a discussion, more like Dan's sermon about what the good book, the only book, has to say about things like this.

The star of the show comes out to touch palms with the audience, perhaps with news that there really is room at the inn. I open the window a crack, waiting for sweet proof of Dan's conversion to humanity but he's only come to tell us that there's still a problem: if we slept in the van the sin would still be occurring on Dad's property.

At the edge of holy ground wind blows dust across our beams of light. On the other side of the main road we park on a trail that cuts between two fields of feed corn. I quietly explain to Shelby that visits can be complicated when your whole family is part of a cult. They pray to their god that I will someday be absorbed.

I push buttons at random on Tim's seduction-oriented control panel until tiny Christmas lights begin to flash around the edges of the ceiling. The bed vibrates. "Another One Bites the Dust" booms from the speakers and won't stop until I turn off the ignition.

Up on the roof of the van, the metal creases and pops as we position ourselves in the cool air, our jeans smearing with dust. I collapse on top of her, deadweight exhausted, convinced that I don't want to right now.

In my tired, angry, exiled state, her wriggling finger near my ass isn't going to do it. Putting my hand on her box isn't going to do it. Sucking my fingers while taking the other hand inside her panties and moving against my fingers might do it. Massaging the muscles at the back of my neck—the ones that run on either side of the head—then scratching that same spot gently with her nails while whispering how much she wants me inside her—that's doing it. I'm hard, despite my reluctance, and she begins to unwrap me.

Soon we're at the part where she won't move until I open my eyes. According to her Coles Notes *Kama Sutra,* we're supposed to stare into each other's eyes and somehow—if we can stop ourselves from laughing—it's going to make us cum harder. Spooky Buddha shit and clingy girlfriend-like behaviour: I can see this ending soon.

Later, under a thousand more stars than the city sky shows, I take her into the woods behind the shop to check out the remains of a fort I had built to escape religious persecution. On Sunday mornings Father would call for me while the rest of the family waited in the car. After they were on their way to another boring sermon I'd take the dirt bike out and ride the trails by the river to meet other godless boys who knew what to do with Sunday mornings.

In the shop there's a combine in for maintenance and over in the corner, in a respectfully cleared area, the Corvette, Dan's substitute for oh so many things. A finger drawn down the hood picks up a dainty layer of dust only, not dirt. Inside, mousetraps guard the upholstery.

A xylophone of wrenches, from tiny to huge, hangs off the east wall, the most sacred part of the shop. A loose spanner lying on a work-bench or a bottle of liquid wrench sitting in the paint can section was enough to make Dad explode at me as an example for the hired hand who would quickly make a detailed study of whatever machine part was nearby. I misplace a wrench just to hear the echo of his curses. Shit on the floor is fine in the barn. But this is a shop. Gallons of ATP are used to scour oil stains off the heavy-duty concrete floor that doesn't have a single crack.

Shelby gets down on the crawler and launches herself to the other side of the combine. I drag her back by the foot and give her a torque wrench so she can play mechanic. She unzips her fly. I tug at her jeans, making the metal wheels scratch against the concrete. I tell her it might work better for me if she pretends to be working but she's worried about breaking something.

The wrench slips from her grip, hitting her cheek. She pushes off from the chassis and I bang the back of my head trying to get out of the way. Her mood improves in the cab where she bounces up and down on the air-cushion seat in time to "Hotel California" while I take a closer look at her bruise. I would have looked forward to harvest if she had been the one in the cab, riding up and down the dusty fields, wearing only underwear and sunglasses.

Our visit in the morning is just a courtesy to inform them that we'll meet them at the lawyer's but as we approach the front steps we're ambushed by the smell of a classic country breakfast. Inside, bacon and eggs, pancakes, and a giant pitcher of orange juice in front of our empty place settings seem specifically arranged to erode our resistance. We barely manage to save ourselves for the fine consistency of a fast-food breakfast in town.

Dad picked the low-bidder again. What else can you assume from the wall of baseball pennant flags and the enormous wall-mounted fish decorating his office? My father's words, spoken by a stranger, give legitimacy to a process that doesn't deserve it. Even in death he can make my head bow forward, my shoulders hunch over to protect vital organs from attack. This will be the last time he knows we'll be listening, and sandwiched between the legalese and convoluted power-sharing plans comes his longest speech, the final I-told-you-so, a farewell scolding that no one can interrupt.

A change in the lawyer's tone brings me back from the dusty fish. Possession of the family home, all property and assets to be divided equally between the named siblings. Management of said property to be negotiated between Dan and named siblings with Dan having final say on day-to-day operations. Do I have a name? Am I a named sibling?

The lawyer doesn't respond to my question. He looks for something in the boxes of documents and personal items to be divided among the named siblings. He finally uncovers a thick white envelope that he hands to me. It seems that I do have a name. It's written right on the envelope.

For a second I think it's a wad of cash. Saving me a trip to the bank and knowing that I'd blow it all anyway would be rare insight for Dad. It sits in my lap, giving off heat while the others stare at it. It would be tacky to rip it open like a Christmas present but tacky seems expected of me. No hurry, I think, enjoying a rare moment of power over Dan who is actually leaning forward in his seat, preparing to what? tackle me?

I break down and open it, if only to keep the planet spinning.

—Hey, look what I got: a Bible! Oh, and it has an inscription: "This is all the wealth you will ever need."

The family is behind us now, but we're still deep in cult territory. There will be no protection until we cross the mountains and reach the coast. In my hands their cult bible will be recycled, reborn as a Cheerios box or paper towels, just like all the other holy texts dumped on me in a wasted campaign to save me from my life.

Shelby uses it to keep her feet off the shag while the nail polish dries. She seems unsure of what exactly happened back there and questions me like someone who didn't get the moral of the story but is sure there must be one.

—Was it your lifelong dream to be a rancher, farmer, cowboy? Okay, so you missed out on your own little sod patch. So what?

—It wasn't a little patch. You know what a section is, right?

—No. Forty acres and a mule is all I know and I take it that's not very much. How much were you going to get?

—A section is a unit of measurement, one square mile of land. There were a lot of sections. If you ripped one page out of the Bible for every mile driven, Sodom and Gomorrah would be destroyed before we reached the edge of our—their—land.

She looks out across the fields, toward the horizon, where dust from the combines makes a deep red sunset. I pick up the Bible, flip to the beginning, and hand it to her.

My Man of Steel

$800 IS $400 PER LIP, EXCLUDING MY TONGUE. THERE WILL BE no charge for the pussy talk earlier this evening. Why not call it foreplay? Usually, it takes an hour for him to get here from his house, which he has described as being somewhere in Point Grey. I imagine the last flight skimming over the moonlit waters of the Strait of Georgia, buzzing woodchip-hauling tugboats and ferries full of wage-earning grunts. If he's flying Helibus, it will be a Sikorsky S76 equipped with IFR, constructed with some kind of lightweight bonded graphite. Graphite is a naturally occurring carbon. The atomic weight of carbon is 12.011.

I have my own key to this empty studio, which he refers to as the Johnson street property. From the third-floor window overlooking downtown Victoria I can see an ugly red brick wall one block down that might be holding up the Fort Street property. Scanning to the left I see a mechanic's shop which could be the Yates Street property, scheduled for termination then reincarnation as a condo highrise. The light tube on the centre of the ceiling brings out ugliness in the flat white paint, makes an exhibit of a single church-basement chair.

I know Jim but I don't know who Jim is. Jim might occasionally share a golf cart with my father, or pay dues to the same yacht club. One might own the other. He told me to meet him at seven and it's already quarter past, less than fourteen hours before the exam. Shivering with my knees to my chin in the corner of this large room, I've decided to charge him extra for the wait.

Shoes clip against the steps in a rhythm that slows as he reaches the third floor. He hangs the trench coat of France over the chair, unbuckles the belt of Italy and lets the pants of New York fall past his knees as he sits down. He never looks directly at me but when he hears the approaching clack of my heels on the hardwood floor, a defeated sigh suggests that I should put his tiresome sex drive out of its misery. The cold air is cruel to his little friend but I can fix it. I can fix everything. This is what I have become: a repairperson, someone who fixes broken men.

A cheery voice on the news today said that now more than ever women were finding it easier to get a head. This is, at last, a statement I can agree with, holding him, soft in my mouth. My mouth of brace corrected teeth. A mouth full of calcium, 40.08, covalent radius of 1.74, cubic face centered crystal structure, white divalent element of the alkaline earth group.

It's a good thing that this one likes me, or needs me, or whatever. We'll have to do this a few more times this month if I'm ever going to get back into the black. Father is once again displaying his grudge-holding skills by stopping all transfers, electronic, computer, silicon: 28.0855, first ionization potential at 8.151, atomic radius of 1.46, grey, brittle, tetravalent. But this working for money does have raw appeal and getting fucked over for a living seems to be the norm. I feel better when I think of the brilliant whores who went before me.

When he is as full as he will get, I take almost all of him.

The secret is to relax the muscles in the back of your throat. He must think that I've cornered the pleasure market with my mouth and my right hand, stand, land, rand, gold 196.9665. But I'm not the source of his pleasure. It's those who came before, their instruction, direction to ecstasy, the same boys he plays squash with, the same ones who help him cheat on his taxes. I'm the conduit for homosexual fantasies he doesn't know he's having.

I wonder how long until his grunt, his little event. And why do they always pull forward like they're trying to impale my skull, drill into my head, bed, dread, lead 207.2, heat of fusion 4.799, specific heat capacity 0.13.

I've heard that man juice is rich in selenium 78.96, hexagonal crystal structure, electrical conductivity varies with level of illumination. The grip tightens while muscles in his abdomen clutch and his head tries to swim away from his body. Krypton is. Krypton would be. Oh he's coming all right, faster than a speeding bullet but not soon enough. There's krypton in this room, providing the light in that fragile tube. Gaseous, inert. I know I could make this man forget to breathe. Or change the colour of this room with one bite. Spelled backwards would be notpyrk. Erratic breathing. Anyday now. Krypton, krypton, krypton. Come on. Where is Superman when you need him? Finally it comes. The atomic weight of krypton is 83.80.

Exit

I STAND UP AND TURN AROUND BECAUSE THAT IS WHAT I always do. We were travelling together but now are dying alone. We speak and when we speak, whine or whisper, it is to and for ourselves. The subtext of the announcement is that the plane will return to the ground in a way the engineers never intended. Advances against gravity are temporary. Obvious risks must be ignored.

When we are advised we are obedient. We root for belt straps and once we hear the decisive click of that metal tongue we feel a little better about 1000 G forces, fireballs, compaction, sparks igniting fuel, flaps jamming, hillsides and ravines. Seat belts on a plane, I say to you, are like air bags on a space shuttle. This makes you cry every time.

I present the tape recorder as a solution, hanging from my hand, this thing that seems like a good idea but never is. It always surprises you. Sometimes you refuse it. Today you talk the black box silly, describe the most passionate moments of your life with the most mundane words. No one will want to hear your tape. It will rip them apart. It will make them disintegrate.

Through the window I see bright blue, then the fields, then blue and a flash of the sun, and I can't watch but I have to. So the plastic blind goes down, then up, then down again. A man behind me does the same. The gravity of each action is tremendous.

Last night, while flat pools of gas in the wings were filled, men and women touched, poked, traced their hands along the outer skin of this plane. These were people who experienced screaming jets, whirring turbines, creaks and thumps as a language. They felt rivets under fingertips as text, a kind of raised lettering. Sometimes they didn't like what they read. Clear, easy, without emotion, these thoughts with their detached, foreign texture, these feelings, these funny feelings. Four people had funny feelings before this flight:
Raj—a technician
Karen—a mechanic
The person seated in 15E
The person seated in 11A

Last night Karen gave Raj a lift to the terminal. His index finger picked at his thumbnail but he was unaware of this. She almost asked him a question.

I turn towards and into you as I always do. Even with the arm rests up it's not an easy place to join. Sometimes the flip-up trays rattle loose and hit me in the back and always the stewardess is tapping me on the shoulder.
—Any sharp objects? Could you put them in the bag?

By now I know you quite well, stranger. My curiosity an excellent complement to your attention. You grind into my pubic bone, squirming and wriggling. I slip into your tight hot, press you deep into those cushions. Pressed against those cushions. Pinned against. You are arching and shagging into me. Your leg cramps so you swing it past my face to rest on the other one. I am waiting for you to start shaking. But there's this thing that always happens. The mutual becomes exclusive and everything around me is forgotten. The better you feel, the farther you move away. A few seconds before and after our orgasms there is separation, and the fact that we are back moments later, full of warmth and generosity, well, that doesn't matter because you left. I left. We separated and nothing changes that cold event, that gap. I remember who I am with a touch.

This is the thing that always kills me: one of your broken ribs punctures my heart. Our bones and flesh are crushed together and I like that. Here are some things I don't like: someone's intestines in a tree hanging like a Christmas decoration and still steaming, a rescue worker walking around with someone's pinkie stuck in his boot tread.

The last time we crashed, everybody came together in the end. It was fire that joined us, made us all the same. Before that, though, I worked you sweaty and you worked me. You were close, moving faster. I knew you, how you wanted to time it right. I was approaching your ear with my lips. I was almost there. I was getting close to telling you something, really.

Unterseeboot

MONICA DUMPED CARL WHEN THEIR RELATIONSHIP WAS 140 hours old. Carl got a crew cut and grew a scruffy beard to ensure that no other woman would want to lure him in and blow him out of the water. He wanted to erase Monica and all associations. That meant no more two-word seductions, no more short-haired blondes, no more women whose names ended in "a."

After the break-up, he couldn't sleep, lost weight and thought about Monica once every minute. That's 1440 times a day. A week later Carl thought about Monica every fifteen minutes which was ninety-six times a day. It amounted to a 99.9 % reduction in the amount of time spent ruminating over her but there was still room for improvement.

He bought a bottle of gin because they never drank gin together. It was dark and humid in the tiny room and the rain reminded him of night number three when they had sex during a thunderstorm. The image of her face by lightning as she came attacked his brain in weak moments like dawn, or when he went shopping alone, or when he had a stomach ache that was either hunger or love.

Carl's gin-saturated brain didn't recognize the danger of mirrors until he confronted an image of his pale unshaven self, a U-boat commander he had seen in an old movie the night before. Lying on his bed, the half-empty bottle capped with his thumb, he began to think how much he'd like to be a U-boat commander, part of the Kaiser's unseen navy, ejaculating torpedoes that churned frothy wakes on their way to blast fat merchant ships. He felt a little sick, leaning over the edge of the bed to spit, convinced that he should be a U-boat commander, guiding the men to their simple goal of destruction, thousands of kilometres from the nearest woman. At 3:30 AM, with the room spinning out of control, silent explosions of light gave way to blind spots in his vision and then dreamless murky black.

Karl lifted his head off the chart to discover that he had drooled all over Scapa Flow, his saliva flooding British naval headquarters there, capsizing the entire fleet. There was a noise over the diesels—not a loose hatch, not a dropped wrench. A piece of a noise, wisp, something different from the usual *Unterseeboot* sounds of humming electrics, clanging doors, waves slapping against the hull. Something was creaking on its hinges somewhere on the boat but he was in no hurry to find it. He considered climbing to the con to chat with the boys on watch but going outside and getting fresh air meant that he would have to descend into the pit again and experience, as if for the first time, the smells of oilskins wet with salty water, moulding mattresses, ripe crewmen, and diesel fumes that hung in his hair.

Passing through the galley, he scraped green mould off a sausage with a knife. He wandered off, munching on his snack, hoping to find the offending noisemaker so that he could blame the appropriate crewman at the beginning of the next shift. It sounded like a voice, this high-pitched creaking, and it was getting louder. By the time he approached the crew quarters he had ruled out anything mechanical, guessing that the thumb-sucking cook was dreaming about his mother being buried in the rubble again.

Karl popped his head through the hatch and choked on a little piece of meat when he saw the young naked woman crying out as she straddled one of the crewmen, shunting his bunk against the hull. His hands were planing over the sweat on her back and then cupping her breasts. Everyone else was asleep, including the man in the attached bunk who was so close he might as well have been a participant.

—*Hör sofort auf!*

She stared at the commander before springing off the crewman, running down the deck plates in the direction of the pumps. When Karl lost her near the forward torpedo tubes he stopped for a few moments to recover, wondering whether this was something that was really happening, something he would remember in the morning.

Scheisse! He wasn't *that* drunk. He had almost touched her. Karl ran back to the crew quarters, falling a few times and bumping his head into the bulkhead once. Predictably, the man who'd had sex with the girl had straightened himself up and was pretending to sleep along with the other angels. Did he think the commander would be too drunk to remember who it was? Karl picked up a wrench and banged it against a pipe.

—*Wachet auf, ihr Faulpelze!* There's a woman loose on the boat. Find her and bring her to me. You three search aft as far as the stern torpedo tubes. You, check from the ventilator to the con. You, the battery room. The rest of you look from the pumps forward.

When they found nothing he ordered another search. Concerned looks passed between the officers, and when Karl walked through the engine room, the mechanics paused to smile. Or were they smirking? No doubt, everyone was a little concerned that the commander was sinking into *Blechkoller*—tin-can neurosis.

For the next three nights Karl engaged in frequent consultations with a case of brandy in his room. Who was she, why was she, was she? Was she servicing the entire crew? In the past few days he had seen more sly smiles and heard more whistling than on the day they set out from Kiel. Why had she not come to *his* cabin?

Instead of running from his room to the crew quarters when he heard the noises, he flooded his body with liquor that gave him peace for a few quiet minutes before he passed out. His searches were futile, although sometimes he would see a flash of her blonde hair just past the diesels, or long legs out of the corner of his eye as she scrambled up the con from the control room. Capture didn't seem likely as she had become acutely aware of his movements and the crew could not be trusted.

If the officers had wanted to mutiny, they could have done so then. Karl knew he was useless, wandering around the ship, picking up the scent of the mystery girl on handles, levers and wheels, dividing his time between cabin sulking and endless inspections.

He left Otto in command, hoping that the eager officer would take over by force. Karl left a wake-up call for anything sighted over ten thousand tons. He would have been relieved if Otto had burst into his cabin, waving his sidearm and shouting orders but he was a disappointment in his loyalty to the commander. Otto could have been the Kaiser's patriotic poster boy, a broad-shouldered wide-smiling submariner, willing to die like a rat in a sinking cage.

He had taken over, but smoothly, quietly, gaining the confidence of the men while assuring the commander of his loyalty. The commander needed assistance and Otto was there to give it. Karl was propped up when he stumbled, guided when lost, cared for as if he were a child.

At night Karl suffered as the wailing echoed through the boat. He tried putting a pillow over his head. He tried reviewing his log, dry details on his twenty-six victims, cargos of cocoa beans, tires, and tin. All the overturned lifeboats he had righted, all the chocolate and brandy and blankets he had provided to those stricken crews, all those gallant actions couldn't recharge his enthusiasm for a war that had become less polite.

He slept lightly through the morning until a watchman reported a convoy of merchant ships, lightly guarded, emerging from the fog. Karl picked a straggler at the back and brought his U-boat much closer than usual, firing two torpedoes at five hundred metres. He thought of all the men below him, labouring blindly like miners while his eyes widened with greed, took in the explosions, watched the ship list to port.

Before he could descend from the con, Otto alerted him to the presence of two corvettes, blocking escape on both sides. Karl had failed to anticipate or even notice the arrival of the ships that were waiting to drop their charges as the boat turned to avoid the sinking ship. Otto swung the periscope from side to side, trying to determine which ship might be slower, carrying fewer charges. The commander saw him then as a boy looking for a way to dump his subtly acquired responsibility. Every second they waited the boat was slicing towards the ship that was spilling its cargo of barrels into the sea.

—Which way, Otto asked, left or right?

—Neither, Karl replied. *Tauchen.* Flood the tanks. We will go under the ship before it sinks, into the heart of the convoy.

The crewman looked to Otto for some kind of override but when none came he was forced to shout the crazy instructions down the voice tube. Flood. Dive. Go to electric. Full power.

Karl took a last look at the ship that was taking on water quickly. They were almost underneath it. The first barrel hit, then more, clanging off the hull, rattling the crew. If the con didn't snag the ship, they would make it under.

This was the moment Karl had often imagined. If the ship came down on top of them the lights would go out. For a time there would be nothing, no sound, no light, before the roar of freezing black water flooded the boat. All crew would then be free to float about at their leisure, finally released from service. The barrels sounded like heavy fists hammering away at the boat, trying to split it wide open.

Carl surfaced slowly as the thumping sound from above grew louder. Somebody was hitting the floor above his apartment screaming shut-up, shut-up, shut-up. During the night the window had fallen shut, trapping dead wet air. Carl's sweat had soaked through the sheet to the mattress, reviving a trace of Monica's scent.

He pulled up the old window as far as it would go, sucking in the air, sucking, sucking until his lungs were full, then the rest of his body, losing its ballast, almost lighter than air. Fresh breeze rushed past him with its endless capacity for cleansing wounds, restoring appetites, carrying with it hope and the vague possibility of survival.

Never Say Tomorrow Dies with Love

FOR TWO WEEKS I LIED ABOUT MY WORKLOAD, PLAYING OFF one side of the office against the other to create the perception that I was in great demand. I wandered from station to station, copying here, filing there, using my down-time in a way that would have made the temp agency proud.

I had almost given up on pulling out any useful information when I found a pink sticky note stuck to the inside of the recycling box Sharon had asked me to empty. Someone had written: *Sharon: Pls. file these in the cabinet under "merger plan."* The "cabinet" referred to a four-drawer lateral filing cabinet at Sharon's station.

I became Sharon's little helper, an excellent position for someone who wanted to peek at her emails and documents or find out where she kept the key to the cabinet. While I was helping Sharon with the reorganization of her library I was also helping myself to highly confidential documents related to the merger plan. It was hard not to laugh when reading memos from executives to the business development group that stressed the importance of secrecy and highlighted the possible destructive effects of a leak.

At 3:30 PM I had an opening. Sharon, the guardian of all things confidential, left early, as soon as the original plan was couriered. Kraig, whose office is adjacent, went skiing up at Whistler with his family.

It's now 4:48 PM on my last day here, and the only hard-copy of the plan, besides the one that's just been couriered to Germany, is being fed through a high-speed copier, causing the competitive advantage of the corporation to erode at one point two five pages per second. The sea has parted and there's nothing ahead but dry sand all the way to the other side.

Allisa bustles into the copy room with the contents of a three-inch binder. She wants to cut in, but I explain that I'm working on a rush job for Roger that'll take about fifteen minutes. Her face shoots a little hate my way as she strides away, the rush of air blowing a loose page off the counter. Moments later she's back, fussing with the pages in the output tray. Seconds hang as she stares directly at one of Roger's notes from the meeting.

—Allisa, I really don't want to get the order of those mixed up, so if you don't mind. . . .

—Oh, right, sorry. I was just checking to see if it was still streaking. I did a big job this afternoon and had to throw out about four hundred sheets. The one downstairs is a lot better.

At the document drop last week my contact Greta wore a beret to cover the effects of chemo. She looked tiny as she stood next to the giant pendulum, waiting for me. I guessed the thing was a pendulum although sometimes it looked like a modern, clean guillotine, ready to slice off heads at two-second intervals. She spotted me, nodded slightly and rode the elevator to the twen-ty-fourth floor. I followed five minutes later, adhering to the new paranoia-inspired drop meet protocol. It was our unit's response to the growing number of companies that had dumped their dopey rent-a-cops in favour of anti-espionage consultants. We stood together at the end of the hall, looking down at the silent, slow traffic as she reviewed my performance: the unit loved the work I was doing. They were very enthusiastic about the material I'd gathered and wanted me to double my production, concentrating on anything to do with the merger.

I told her that I was going to have to bill her extra for all the paper cuts I had endured. I showed her a really nasty one on the webby part between my thumb and forefinger. Oh my poor dear, was what she said as I handed her the latest batch of documents.

That day her loving lecture was about money. Long-term disability and pension plans weren't things that I probably knew about but there would come a day when I felt their absence. Right now it might seem important to have a wall of CDs but later that might not seem like a wise investment. Many people still think that they will be taken care of when they become weak.

We stood together for a few more minutes looking down at the cars. I glanced at her out of the corner of my eye, alarmed by the way her skin stuck tightly to the bones of her face. I asked her, as I always did, if there was anything I could do for her. She said, as she always did, no.

Jackie has been looking all over for me. I move between her and the copier. When I turn to face her maniacal grin, she pulls Daniel's latest finger painting from behind her back. A gift to thank me for the tickets. Stick people with smudgy labels. Barney, I think, and all his wild kingdom friends painted inaccurately but cheerfully, using the full Crayola spectrum. Daniel would like it very much if I came over for dinner sometime.

—That's me, that's Daniel, and that one, the tall one with the gigantic shoes? that one's you. We're together, over here.

—Actually, it looks like I'm closer to the animals than I am to you guys.

In retrospect, free tickets to Barney was a mistake. Jackie was thrilled, leaning over to kiss my cheek, but that was nothing compared to how her son latched on to his new reason to live. According to Jackie, he woke up at 3:00 AM on the morning of the show and by the time they were sitting in the arena with five thousand other screaming, squirming, wriggling kids, he was close to combustion. A man in a purple foam suit came onto the stage and every little mouth let out the memorized words of the feel-good anthem.

It was futile to explain to her that the tickets meant nothing. They had been given to me, and the only person I could think of who could use them was her. It wasn't an expression of interest in her or her child.

It was just like the time she caught me cleaning her workstation. I wasn't being nice. I just couldn't stand being that close to her grub factory anymore. There were so many crumbs under the letters of her keyboard, it looked like someone had crumbled a piece of toast over it. The home keys were greying, on their way to being black with dirt and finger acid. I didn't have the guts to even look at the earpiece on her phone. Her screen was spotted with fingerprints and the back of her monitor was covered in dust. She assumed my efforts were part of some mating ritual, a display by the male indicating ability to clean, comfort with domestic chores.

If I enjoyed constant cleaning I'd follow Tanya around my apartment with a dust buster and a garbage bag. Tanya, whom I've mentioned to Jackie a hundred times or so, doesn't even live with me but you wouldn't know that if you saw my place.

In the beginning a box under the bathroom sink held her toiletries, and order was maintained. Soon after, chaos revealed itself as a blow dryer on the counter, a single hairpin near the baseboard or a brush filled with hair on the kitchen table.

Minutes after she had entered my apartment for the first time, she began a close investigation.

—You have a lot of Bond films.

—I have all the Bond films.

—He's such a misogynist though.

—Irrelevant. He has a job to do.

—But having sex with all those women isn't part of the job. He rarely uses them for information. One after another, he fucks 'em and kills 'em. He's just not a very good person.

—Whatever. They're still classic films.

—You mean classic in a *Plan 9 from Outer Space* kind of way?

She took a silent hour to scan my CD collection and when she was finished there were no questions about the obscurity of some of the bands or the extremely rare imported labels. She sat down on the couch, let out a huge sigh and stared out the window. I countered by grabbing her purse off the table and exposing her bad purse habits. There were too many credit cards. A few could go missing and she wouldn't realize it until weeks later. The SIN card and birth certificate are used so infrequently that they shouldn't be carried. A thief would be thrilled with her complete ID package, worth about a hundred bucks on the street.

The rest of the purse was a stalker's resource kit. There were pictures of the family, an old phone bill with the numbers of all her out-of-town friends neatly itemized. It was full of opportunities, especially the passwords section at the back, for easy access to her email, gym, even her bank and credit cards. Old Visa bills matched her up to favourite restaurants and shops, excellent locations to stake out for pictures or the simple pleasure of close contact.

This week she's leading an invasion of privacy which she calls "getting to know me." So I tell her: Do you really want to know more about my childhood? When I was twelve my father thought it was time for me to learn about sex. We drove to the East Side and picked up a young hooker. He asked her what kind of music she liked while we walked together from the parking lot into the woods. She was paid to kiss me and I seemed very enthusiastic about that, so, at my father's instruction, she moved on to oral sex. There wasn't much hanging around after that. Dad had to fly a 747 to Singapore. The girl seemed busy too, walking away quickly without a backward glance. On the way back to the car my father told me that some girls would do that for free. It was an education of sorts but it didn't really explain anything. Every year there were more questions.

Last Wednesday I came home and found a new couch and an area rug in my living room. Did she think my place was spare because I just hadn't the time to fill it with junk? I was sitting in the dark on her couch when she came in, expectant and happy.

—This is nice, but it has to go back.

When Mark's heels hit the copy room floor I wheel around to block the feed tray from his view. After I've worked in his section for two months he finally knows my name and uses it often, with confidence.

—Hey, you've already impressed us. I know you're the hardest working temp in Vancouver but you don't have to work like a maniac all the time. Look at you. You're sweating!

Mark lets me know that the extra effort has not gone unnoticed. The long hours, a good work ethic: these were things they looked for in their employees. There might be a full-time position opening up in records management. I might want to bring in my resumé. He'd have HR look it over and who knows? He's proud to offer this and happy for me too as if he's just offered me partnership in the firm. I hope to at least look enthusiastic as the muscles in my jaw clench and unclench, a stretched, toothless smile doing its best to transmit the right message.

Lillian arrives and drives Mark away with her big sulky presence. My explanation about the rush job has repelled so many others, but it isn't working on her. She glares from the far side of the room. Her hands come up on her hips, creating a massive, unmovable barricade that blocks the exit.

—I know what you're doing. You're so obvious. You're not going to get my job because I have ten years' experience. If they hire you permanently you'll have to work under me.

—You don't have to worry about that, Lillian. I'm sure they would never hire me at a higher level than someone who has been here for ten years. You're the pro. You're the document pro here, and I'm sure everyone knows that.

5:05 PM. I haul my sagging gym bag back to my station through the empty office. Linda, a five o'clock sprinter, has left the database open again. Usually I would take a free meal at the information buffet but not today, not in the last minutes. If I wanted to I could see how many employees use the names of pets for their password or how many keep it on a sticky note in their top drawer.

I take the stairs to avoid reception. The heavy thud of the fire door behind me is confirmation that I'm out now, safe. On the street, well-dressed people with pensions begin their mad scramble for home, past me, around me, hot and frustrated by my pace.

Toronto, soon. It's only a rumour but Greta is usually right.

She and I will move with the rest of our unit, and then it won't matter that I'm starting to bump into too many people that I know from other jobs.

Home feels like a crime scene and I'm the first cop to step carefully through, wide-eyed at every detail. A lot of things look suspicious. The hardwood floor is dust free but half a sandwich and a glass of milk have been left on the kitchen counter for the silverfish. There's no dust on the top of the fridge or the oven vent, no crumbs on the floor but a dish rag rots in the kitchen sink. The clean, classic aesthetic ends with a jolt in the bedroom where a gigantic stuffed ape sits on the bed.

Kong came from a dart thing at the PNE that Tanya made me try. I popped a few balloons and then we were parents. We took our ape home and argued immediately about how it would be raised. Tanya spoiled him by letting him sleep on the bed, which he seemed to dominate. I felt it was best to remind him often of his subordinate position to humans by stuffing him up onto the top shelf in the closet.

We were fighting last night. She was yelling at me about this or that and all I could think about was the note I was going to leave. Clean, simple, lying on the floor of my clean, simple apartment. Just enough to prevent her from reporting me as a missing person but not so much that she'll guess where I've gone or why.

She walks in and picks up where we left off last night.

—How come you never tell me about your work?

—Then you would know too much. SPECTRE would send assassins and I would have to protect you.

—Why do you always have to joke about it? Why can't you tell me the truth? You're a dial-a-doper, aren't you? That's the reason you vacuum so often: it's because of the powder. If they ever brought dogs in here they'd bark their heads off. I don't care what you do. I'm just hurt that you won't tell me.

Two weeks later the first part of the note comes from memory, from all the other times. The postscript comes after an hour of spinning the pen through my fingers.

PS.   A soft thud from the bedroom. Kong has jumped to his death again. He's too full of life to be contained in the place I have made for him. Too full of life and mischief, like you.

The File Lady

THE FLIGHT ATTENDANT REACHES OVER MY ROW-MATES WITH another gin and tonic and I take it without explaining my tears. I could tell her it's the altitude combined with sappy music on the earphones and raging nostalgia for old girl-friends but I know she wouldn't care. The screaming child up front needs attention.

The woman next to me might relax if I told her it's normal for me, I'm not upset. She strains against her seatbelt, turning away from me because I am a man in a suit, typing and crying. Don't pity me, I want to say. These are my best hours, when I'm moving but not moving, out of reach and fixed on my task. I don't even remember dinner being served. By the time I raise the blind to take a break, I'm staring at the surprisingly green Pacific Ocean.

I follow Julie's body around the office, smiling and joking with people I have met two or three times on previous floor tours.

They ask about my shop and how the project is going and I'd like to do the same but can't fake interest in someone I don't remember. Thankfully, Julie is new and can't say things like, "You remember Bob from Justice?" Or worse, "Have you met Bob?" If I remember Bob's name I'll say "Hello, Bob." If I can remember anything else about Bob I might mention that, but Julie seems committed to doing things properly, squinting at the floor map before the next set of introductions is made and forgotten.

Turns out Julie is only an IS3, a junior officer with less than eight months' experience in the department. She's the one they chose to escort me (a job usually done by the Director General) after I'm flown out to Vancouver on five hours' notice, a week ahead of schedule to deal with a Code Red emergency.

Before I left Ottawa, Millar had taken over Skeena, which could blow apart any day due to the protests. As a favour to him before I left, I debriefed him in detail, showed him where the traps were, and all he did was nod and smile, as if it were obvious.

On my way down to the cafeteria I pass by Records to check on the stack of K-48s I dropped off this morning. When asked about the forms, which seem to be untouched, the file lady pushes them toward me, points to the red "X" in Section D and goes back to two-finger typing.

Julie and I indulge the clerk by filling out the blank sections, making sure we conform with Federal procedures. It takes over an hour to look up all the filing codes and provide detailed descriptions of each file based on our requirements and the letter of the form. Halfway through this the ADM calls me. After six trials, three meetings and one blown-off intro, this is our first conversation. He wants to chat, saying stupid Easterner things about West Coast weather, how lucky I am to be there, etc. I wait for news of the crisis, the media slip, the change in strategy that does not come. He ends the call because he has to go to a meeting. An excuse to end the call quickly? Why call then? To show that he is an important, busy person. To fill time before a meeting. He was sitting there in the board room and none of his colleagues had shown yet. He felt silly sitting there alone so he called me and ended it as soon as someone he knew showed. Or the Deputy Minister asked him to check up on me.

Julie's an instant admirer when I tell her who it was. She touches my forearm when she asks what he's like. Well...he has a lot of European hooker stories, he brags constantly about his golf game and prides himself on the staff burnout rate in his office. He gave his wife syphilis last year as a birthday present and he can't spell. Impressed yet? Of course, she doesn't believe me.

I leave a message with Millar and go down to face the file lady again, this time with Julie, who tries a softer approach, similar to begging. She jokes and pleads, empathizing about the heavy workload and then there's an apology for asking the file lady to actually do filing. Later Julie explains that the file lady is responsible for initiating twelve different grievances against co-workers and supervisors, almost her entire section. Julie's management has not been grieved.

Our forms have been rejected because they do not conform to the BC Region Policies and Procedures manual, which is an amusing piece of administrative fiction, a daring departure from actual Federal Regs. Julie calls it "slight regional differences in the application of policy." After three hours of accommodating regional differences we bring back the forms only to be rejected again for reasons the file lady will not explain.

A clerk from records comes by to help.

—She likes dogs. Get her one of those picture books about dogs. That's worked for me in the past.

—You mean bribes?

—No, offerings. Others have used Dare Real Fruit

gummies. Make sure it's the Fruit Medley flavour. She hates the other kind.

Back at the hotel, I pour my own, repeat as necessary. Some time after that sleep happens. At 5:00 AM the ADM calls again. There's no apology for the time because he forgot about the time difference or doesn't care. It's 8:00 AM in Ottawa and that's the important thing. He asks how things are going. He must have heard something. Another pointless call with many references to my lucky trip to Vancouver. Because of the weather? this assignment? In five minutes we're done, the project not even mentioned. He didn't ask me because he doesn't want to know. He didn't ask me because he doesn't care. Because he assumes that if there were a problem I would tell him. Because he wants to be able to tell the DM that he called me but wants to make up his own progress report. Because he's an incompetent, forgetful idiot.

In the morning we should feel refreshed, ready to see things differently. Conflicts of yesterday have passed without being examined or understood. Someone who appeared to be an enemy might be an ally.

The person standing over me, the waitress, is saying something, asking if everything is okay. Is it my glazed look or the way I have mashed my fruit salad into a pulp?

First thing, I check for our files at Records where the file lady is on the phone, discussing best practice for getting ticks off a long-haired collie, but she's nice enough to point out the red marks on our requests as she talks.

From Julie's office I watch the barges being towed and float planes landing near the terminal. The ADM calls while I'm tranced out on this big yellow cone of sulphur over in North Van and even as I tell him the necessary lies, my face goes red and I can feel a stickiness around my collar. The entitlements from Records will be coming through shortly. It feels good to say that as if it's just a detail.

Through all of this, Julie persists with questions about my career path, leafing through my planner as if through the Bible, impressed by the names she recognizes from the *Globe and Mail*, the schedule that presses to 11:00 PM every night. I want to ask her, what is wrong with you that you want to do what I do? Does this look like fun? Her dangerous enthusiasm and reckless willingness to work will result, if unrestrained, in further promotions and raises, making departure from the service impossible.

I could use her back east, halt her upward movement before the damage was too great. Together we would rule Regional Coordination, silently, without credit, attracting neither praise nor blame: a perfect sustainable habitat in the Federal eco-system.

The deadline for submissions to the Supreme Court is on Friday. If every available member of legal counsel worked on the project it would take two days to review the documents and prepare our submission. The ADM is faxing every hour, not to put the pressure on, oh no, just to make sure that I realize it's a $400 million claim. No pressure, just a friendly reminder that this one's pretty important.

The file lady smirks at me now every time I pass the counter. You know, if I wanted to ruin someone, this is how I would do it: I would send them away, have someone take over their files, stick them with impotent people and watch their career die of embarrassment. She is smirking. Probably has Millar and the PCO on her speed dial. And what about Julie, always with me, documenting my incompetence in her Harvard Planner, for another kind of trial perhaps.

—Hi, Linda. How's Millar doing with Skeena?

—Good. He's a real take-charge kind of guy. He's printing out a whole pile of stuff off your drive so he can work at home.

—He's on my M drive? Linda, none of the Skeena files are on my M drive. You know that. Listen, I want you to lock out access to that drive. And change my password.

—But if it's changed he's going to know who did it.

—That's fine. Just tell him I told you to do it. Can you do that for me?

—I guess. Why don't you tell me what's happening? Maybe Millar can help.

—I'll pass on that. But have him call me. It's important.

Julie has promised to solve our file problems while I work on the phrasing of the email I will probably have to send to the ADM.

I can't get a CR4 to cooperate with my request for records. A postponement is extremely unlikely, considering our history with this judge. If things don't improve we may lose this one. Hope things are going well on your end.

Julie and I discuss options because I want to be sure that she knows what this means. Four zero zero, zero zero zero, zero zero zero. When I show her the faxes from the ADM she begins to pick at her nail, biting off loose tags of skin.

A year ago I attended a party that the Minister held to thank me for my involvement in the Kitimat trial. I had a chance to see the ADM and DM, who had been whipping me all year, both stop their chewing for a moment when I arrived with a date from PCO. The Minister had invited me personally without mentioning it to anyone else.

Now they thank me by sending Millar, career assassin and gifted bootlicker, trying on my job while I'm in Vancouver grovelling to a CR4. The "p.s." in an email from the ADM states that Millar is now my special liaison. Who won't answer my calls.

—Is Millar in the office?

—Yes, he's in.

—Why won't he return my calls?

—He's quite busy with meetings today. Would you like his voicemail?

—No, I want you to take a paper message and staple it to his fucking forehead. Thank you.

The group standing in my office may be the support team I had expected when I first arrived. Something may have happened last night, a profound event that motivated and excited my colleagues, big questions followed by revelations that caused them to question old methods, issues, even their self-definitions. But I doubt it.

The box on my desk is the star of the show. It holds my planners, notes, phone, laptop, phone book, tag list. Everyone leaves except Julie and Cathy. The file lady has filed harassment charges. I have "intimidated" her with my overly aggressive, "threatening" manner. Two commissionaires stand ready to escort me out. Julie will take over my duties and complete the project. I may communicate with Julie by email but I may not return to the building until the investigation is complete.

The elevator opens on the ground floor and I move toward the doors. I carry my sad box of things between an escort of elderly guards who let me take the last steps on my own. The wind flips my tie over my shoulder and works its way between the buttons of my shirt. It's good to be out on a sunny morning with nowhere to go and nothing to do.

Down near the rowing club in Stanley Park, I sit on a bench and watch the float planes take off. I stare at the boats in the marina and tear the ADM's latest fax in half, quarters, eighths that fly into the bay, briefly examined then rejected by a gull.

Julie calls and orders me to meet her at the office at 9:00 AM. I don't tell her that I'm no longer interested in pathetic attempts to complete the K-48s in a way that will appease the file lady, that by now probably involves multicoloured pens or circles over the "i"s with little happy faces in them.

I will shower and shave and cab it over there because in the nine hours since last contact I have forgotten what Julie looks like, the shape of her lips, the way the colour of her blouse affects her eyes. Nine hours since she has stolen one of my pens, lost it and reached for another.

She comes from inside and surprises me with a tap on the shoulder. She tugs me into the building, holding my arm a little longer than necessary. Or as long as necessary to stabilize an old man. The second physical contact in case I didn't catch the significance, the intention of that tap on the shoulder. Or none of the above, with no meaning or significance to the taps, touches and grasps as they all fall within acceptable parameters for non-sexual contact. But Feds don't touch, haven't touched in fifteen years.

On the way up I ask her about the scraps of wriggly paper shreds in her hair. She had hopped over the file lady's counter and hidden in one of the recycling bins until closing in order to gain access to the file room.

Our white board is covered with different-coloured lines, circling each other, doubling back, pointing to nothing, or out into space. We find the maps stacked in a bunch of tote boxes next to the shredder, in no particular order. One hour later

Julie discovers they are filed by scale first, then region. I get a really bad paper cut while trying to find a pattern to the documents section. I've tried it by date, order date, filing date, alpha order, numerical order, by judge, clerk of the court, geographical location and the name of the band.

We break at 10:30 PM and I succumb to Julie's pizza suggestion. We're getting the Greek veggie special and as she dials I hand her a note with the critical instruction: "*sliced* tomatoes *on top* of the cheese." She gives that exact instruction without even seeing my note.

She lies on her side on the table eating her pizza while I sit in the chair. Her everything is close to my face. She smells good. I wouldn't notice that unless she were moving closer. She may be looking at me when I'm not looking at her. When she does something useful for me she seems to shine. Or I flatter myself. Or she's just a night person.

She's close again, asking about this or that, something I respond to without thinking, tense in the left half of my body, trying to avoid brushing against her as I want to, twisting away slightly from that contact.

The clutter of computers, printers and tote boxes seems to help counter the distraction of having Julie in my hotel room until her arm contacts my shoulder as she reaches over me to get more staples. She could have gone to the other side, reached the staples without even coming close. Then, after she spends a long time in the washroom, it looks as if she re-applied her make-up.

Our HQ nest is comfortable enough but the maps take up room, forcing Julie to spread some of the material out on her bed. Soon after she is sitting on the bed, scanning and sorting the material, then lying on her side because it is more comfortable and she is tired, would like to rest her body if she cannot rest her mind. I lean back in my chair, resting my feet on her bed.

Close to morning I think I should join her on the bed as soon as I have a good question, one that requires closeness, to point out what I mean, one that can't be answered quickly so I must stay and explain. I lie back on my bed and stare at the same graph for five or ten minutes thinking of involved, dry issues like revenue variance or the capital re-investment adjustment. Fatigue has erased all boundaries and distinctions and the paper that surrounds us seems like a disguise that's getting boring. Julie seems to want to continue this game, pretending to be fascinated by a map of the watershed, tracing her finger down the dry paper into the centre crease.

When I wake up Julie is sitting on the edge of the bed with the notebook on her lap, looking at the trial schedule. Her eyes, at least, look in that direction. I ask her something and she doesn't respond, then breaks suddenly from her trance. She shovels everything off her lap and lies down for a moment. Before I can finish my pitch for a room service breakfast her head is set into the pillow, her breathing deep.

There is no note, business or personal, when I return. The maid has not yet come and Julie's bed is as she left it, the sheets twisted and creased from her weight, her pillow still carrying perfume and a few of her hairs.

The commissionaires are old, not likely to remember the face of a guy they escorted down the stairs last week. With baseball cap and sunglasses I walk by their station looking purposeful. I'm past the desk before I hear hollering behind me. Someone points and I run five flights of stairs to Julie's office, locking the door and closing the blinds before the knocking and yelling begins.

—Would you come to Ottawa with me?

—When?

—Now.

—In what capacity?

—As my partner.

—You mean there could be two Regional Coordinators within the department? Do they have enough PYs for another position?

On the plane my jaw aches from clenching as the scene in her office cycles. We stared at each other and waited for the other to speak.

Julie and I will live in Kerrisdale where everyone's lawn looks like the green on a golf course. A third-floor white stucco apartment building with a few well-chosen possessions. And although we will take turns making gourmet meals with organic vegetables, there will also be frequent dinners at a neighbourhood restaurant (Greek perhaps) where we will become known and spoiled.

We will have one rotary black phone with no answering machine or service. Often, one of us will even answer it and talk for hours about nothing, twirling the phone cord on a finger until day turns to night.

On rainy days we will be forced to stay inside under the heavy duvet. The cat will infiltrate our feather cave, gaining access by one of the side tunnels. On weekend mornings there will be few reasons to leave the bed. My face will travel the length of her, gathering textures, tastes and smells. Time will be measured vaguely by the progress of the sun as it moves across each board of the dark-stained floor.

All this and more I have foreseen, jetting through space, typing my report, crying.

Travel Tips for the Desperate

No maintenance payments? No access. Maris likes to summarize complex situations with stupid little quips. If she can sum it up in a few words it can't be that complex, right? Sometimes it amuses me to describe my own life in this way. No job? No food in fridge.

Maris thinks I arranged to be laid off to get out of paying child support. Yeah. Choose poverty. To her all my reasons are excuses and nothing I say can be accepted at face value. She doubts that my so-called layoff was caused by a so-called restructuring brought on by the so-called recession.

I am currently hauling my so-called layed-off ass across the great state of Texas. I am singing with

TIP 1—FREE RIDE

If you don't think your car can make the trip, borrow someone else's. Don't tell them you're taking it to Texas. Tell them you're picking up your grandmother from the airport. If it's an older vehicle, approach it with confidence. Old cars sense fear. Don't go on a road trip if you can't stop worrying about threadbare tires, the brakes that need pumping or an engine that makes strange noises. Any beater can survive a road trip. There's no reason to think that a few thousand more kilometres will kill it. Never coddle a vehicle to avoid a breakdown. Shift hard, rev high, and dive into those exit ramps at your usual speed. You are in control.

Madonna as loud as I can. She is keeping me awake as I fire through Houston. On the freeway, bright lights and flashes enter the corner of my eye as I pass over a million lives without taking one look.

Three hours later I'm lured down an exit by signs promising food and gas. The car adjusts nicely to slower speed but I find it unnerving, creeping through the empty streets of this nothing town. Once again I've missed the welcome sign at the edge of town. There are no clues to suggest a name and no one on the street to ask if I were to really care. Nothing. Welcome to Nothing. I wonder how often comatose interstate travellers like me fall asleep at the wheel cruising Nothingville and drive into immovable objects.

I pull into a gas station, shut off the engine and sit for a moment in the silence, so strange after a six-hour stretch on the road. It's hot here, even in the middle of the night. Moths circle a humming light. I step into the machine-cooled air and troll the shelves of junk food. One clerk is telling the other about the outrageous events of last night's party. I grab some chips and a Pepsi and, feeling generous, decide to pay for everything, even the gas. One hundred seventy-three dollars remaining.

The car smells and this time it's not mechanical problems. Something is growing on the backseat under a pile of hamburger wrappers, milkshake containers, paper bags, and stray fries that have greased their way into the rug. The floor in the back is probably wet—all those drive-through drinks loaded to the top with ice to complement the trace elements of the drink I ordered.

Three sharp cracking knocks on the window wake me, my shirt wet from the heat of the morning sun, my head booming. I stare into the belly and eventually the face of a policeman. I feel like puking. Everything ends here. I eventually remember that I have not yet committed a crime.

The officer leisurely examines my licence, mentioning a complaint received from the manager of the daycare where I am parked. He seems a little disappointed that I'm clean. I'm sure he'd much rather find an open beer bottle or a baggie of smack, just to confirm his impressions of me. I move off the lot after explaining that I took the wrong turn off the freeway, got lost, and was too tired to drive any further. The screwed-up face of a woman behind the glass door of the daycare turns away when I return her stare. In an hour the parents will start dropping off the children.

When I return it's already mid-morning. The staff scramble to their battle stations to block my entrance, their faces wired shut with resolve. Guess I should have shaved—and showered. These small thorny women make it obvious that I'm not getting access to the centre. Someone in the background is being told to call the police.

> **TIP 2—FREE GAS**
>
> Never rush through a driveaway. Take your time, wash the windows, check the oil. Wait for the right activity level—two cars that pull in at the same time, for example. They might run after you but it's a token effort. Clerks and gas jockeys don't really care.

I call Kelly's name into the hallways, over the sound-absorbent barriers. She pushes her way through a fence of legs and runs into my arms, screaming with excitement. The woman on the line to the police pauses, then hangs up.

I try to leave with Kelly but the staff surround me. I pull out a wrinkled piece of paper, my court order, certified true by the court clerk, certified by ketchup in a diner in Omaha, certified by coffee in Fort Worth. The document, listing the details of my access during summer months, seems to relax them somewhat. Their knot loosens enough so that the path to the door is clear. I haul Kelly into the heat, with a few staffers following me, pleading, warning, lots of information about what I can't do. I back away from the curb and notice one of the woman scribbling notes on her pad, probably jotting down the out-of-state licence as I drive away.

I keep wondering how far away I am and if it's far enough.

San Antonio has long since disappeared from the mirror. Kelly's rapid-fire interrogation has slowed to one question every five minutes. She rolls up her window and urges me to do the same in order to keep the car cool. I try to explain that the car doesn't have air conditioning but she won't believe me, insisting that every car has it. We try it her way, ten minutes with the windows up, suffering in a smelly sauna before she breaks down and rolls her side down.

Around lunchtime she becomes sullen. She wants to know where we're going, what's going on, sliding into a W5 routine, questions I can't answer. She squirms in the seat to get a look out the back window and starts crying that she wants her mommy. I reach out to her in an attempt to calm her but she squirms away from my touch. People stare as they pass the car with the bawling kid and the stone-faced father. They must wonder what kind of nut would take a car without air-conditioning across Texas in summer.

> **TIP 3—FREE FOOD**
>
> Eat 3/4 of burger. Select dead bug from dead bug collection. Embed dead bug into remaining portion of burger. Loudly spit out portion of partially chewed burger. Become furious and complain to management. Receive full refund. If out of bugs, use broken glass or staples.

An hour later the child is still crying. I wonder how long before dehydration becomes an issue. She shows no sign of slowing down. As the sun is setting, I feel like an ogre, wondering how much longer this can go on. I don't know what to do. I try to solve things with food but highway fare doesn't please Kelly.

—We can't go there. That's where poor people eat.

When I can't take it any more, I turn down an exit, following a sign that promises lodging. The faded sign of The El Dorado is framed with promises of decadence: colour TV, pool, and a sauna, something I could probably do without. The refrigerated room is a full twenty-degree drop. Kelly seems to come to life again, using one of the beds as a trampoline. I didn't know that kids still did that. One hundred twenty dollars remaining.

I fall asleep in my clothes. When Kelly shakes me into consciousness an hour later, it takes some time for me to orient myself. She has to brush her teeth: it's a rule. Luckily the vending machine near the pool offers a toothbrush and toothpaste. One hundred seventeen dollars remaining.

In the morning I spread the map out on the bed. We are in Texarkana, a little town that borrows the names of the states it straddles. I'm trying to figure out if we're still in Texas or if the hotel room is in Arkansas, out of reach of the Texas police. The cross over would mean that Phase 1 is complete.

I worry about the whining. It's going to be hard to travel with her if that is a constant feature. We won't be able to have much contact with the public if she's whining about her mother. Anyone could act on that. Anyone would. I could take her back. That would be simplest. Her fit may have just been fatigue. She does seem more relaxed around me now. I'd like to explain, show her the order, my legitimate claim to her, but it all seems a little ridiculous.

In the restaurant she behaves much better than I had hoped. She entertains me with stories about her friends, plans for school next year. She manages to do a better job of keeping the syrup dispenser clean than I do. Ninety-one dollars remaining.

I tell her we have all day together, to hang around, go out on the town, hoping that is what she wants to hear. First things first: she wants to shop, dragging me to a kids' clothing store in one of the nearest strip malls. The beautiful clerk pays too much attention to us, coming right out and saying that she thinks it's cute, a man taking his little girl out to buy a dress. Kelly starts grabbing things and dragging them to the front counter where the smiling clerk takes them and folds them up for her. When she's done she looks up at me expectantly. I take a look at one of the price tags and then point Kelly toward the door.

—Daddy left his wallet at the motel. Don't worry, we'll come back for these.

I say it as much for the clerk as for Kelly. No one's fooled.
Outside on the sidewalk Kelly pouts.

—Gavin buys me whatever I want.

—Who's Gavin?

—Mommy's boyfriend.

—Uh-huh, and what does Mommy's boyfriend do?

—He takes care of Mommy.

After shopping we go for ice cream where Kelly again shows me up on manners, scowling as I lick a runaway flow of vanilla off my hairy arm. Eighty-eight dollars remaining.

> TIP 4 —FREE PARTS
> Why would anyone buy an auto part—say, a fan belt—when there are perfectly good parts sitting in the parking lot of any mall?

I try to get more information on Gavin.

—What does Gavin do to make money?

—Gavin drives a car.

—He drives a cab? He's a limo driver?

—He drives a race car. And he drives a helicopter. It's black with a red stripe.

When we get back to the motel it's late afternoon and Kelly says she wants to go into the pool. Her mother apparently gave her swimming lessons on a cruise ship.

—We went for a cruise in the Mediterranean. That's where Greece is.

—You've been to Greece?

—Haven't you?

—No.

—Have you been to France?

—No.

—Have you been to Germany?

—No. I haven't been anywhere.

Phase 2 is starting to look not so good. I begin to wonder how Kelly will like the basement suite I'm now sharing with a long-distance trucker. It's not exactly a separate room I've prepared for her but there is a partition for privacy.

Swimming is good, cost-conscious fun. I pick up a bathing suit for her at the mall and luckily it does not offend her highbrow taste. Sixty-eight dollars remaining.

I realize, as I hold Kelly above the water, that she has no reason to lie about knowing how to swim. I lower her to her waist but can't let her go completely. My throat is dry and I'm shaking. My half-submerged daughter is squirming between my two hands, telling me over and over to let go while her small limbs splash in the water. And then I do let go, surprised by the truth, shocked by it, as my child swims all the way across the pool and back to me.

Out of the pool I towel her off, wrap her up and hold her, looking up into the cloudless sky. This holding is very different from the idea of daughter, a picture in my wallet, already out of date.

> TIP 5—FREEWAYS
>
> Freeways are designed for people who are half asleep anyway. That's a given. You might as well take advantage of the foresight of road engineers. When you pass through ordinary fatigue you will enter the ideal driving state in which the body conserves energy by engaging only those muscles and brain functions necessary for driving. The feet are dormant thanks to cruise control. The wheel is directed by minute contractions in the first two fingers and thumb. The seat is in a generous recline and the head lies against the rest, joggled occasionally by bumps on the road. The eyes are open only a crack, just enough to receive the faint input of dotted lines that guide you to your destination.

That night, after Kelly gets over the tiny screen and the lack of a DVD player, we watch *The Little Mermaid* on the movie channel until about nine when I decide it's beddy-bye time. Beddy-bye time—something I have never had the chance to announce to my child.

The storm we heard coming is now upon us and lightning strikes nearby, scaring Kelly. Automatically, she hops from her bed into mine, snuggling up to me, a simple admission of fear. Soon after, she is asleep, wedged against the side of my body. Although I am tired, I have never been able to sleep on my back. I don't have the heart to wake her by moving, so I lie awake, thinking about how I had just made the world safe for my little girl, thinking of how my presence was enough to make thunder and lightning harmless, thinking of how Kelly can swim on her own, thinking of the long drive back to San Antonio.

Taliban Barbie

THERE WAS ONCE A LONELY MAN NAMED LORNE WHO LIVED in a Heritage Building in Vancouver's West End where the gay people lived, not that all people who lived there were gay, not that all the people who were gay lived there. Lorne had many things that other people wanted. A few of his colleagues were after his job as Head of Pediatrics at VGH. Others wanted his huge apartment that overlooked English Bay. Those who looked into his sad eyes often wanted to rescue him, hold his head against their chest and make everything all right. Some glanced at his body as he walked away, checking out his tight, sculpted gluteals, guessing at his dimensions from the way his pants hung.

Lorne knew that the people who wanted what he had did not care about what *he* wanted. Every day Lorne was reminded of what he wanted by couples who put their arms around each other, walked hand-in-hand, kissed at bus stops, and smiled at each other for no particular reason. From the fourth floor of his building he could see many other buildings across the Bay in Kitsilano and he often imagined the loving couples who lived in those buildings.

The clerical support workers in Pediatrics were terrible gossips and not very discreet either—he could hear most of it from his office. He was reasonably sure they knew he was gay but you wouldn't know it from the way they talked. He felt he was being obvious—obvious enough. He wasn't about to put on makeup and do a dance number dressed in ostrich feathers just to clarify things.

He knew they called him Ken because they thought he was a perfect man with a perfect life and he knew that some of them wanted to be his Barbie. Sometimes he was tempted to take one them aside and straighten the whole thing out. He wanted to say, my life is not perfect. My life is shit. In any case, *being* Barbie would be much better than having one. Ken seemed to lack range. Some parents probably passed over Ken altogether for the macho, man-killing G.I. Joe, just to make darn sure their boy didn't turn gay.

As a child Lorne had always admired Barbie's permanent smile, excellent posture, and the outflow of long blonde hair as she drove around in her pink convertible Corvette. She was a well-rounded innovator with a limitless sense of fun who always pushed to expand her experience. He hoped the current Barbie personas were keeping up to the times. He would be tempted to buy them all: Underwater Welder Barbie, Single Mom Barbie, Greenpeace Barbie, NHL Goalie Barbie, Taliban Barbie, and Bomb Squad Barbie.

On Saturday morning Lorne went to Delaney's. On his way down he stopped by the parking garage to visit his car, a black Porsche Boxster that hadn't been driven since the salesman parked it there. It was between a wall and a pillar, for maximum protection from scratches. Lorne pulled his shirt cuff over his hand and buffed a spot on the rear fender, his fingers tracing lightly over the metallic nameplate. The engine revved with the promise of power and the airy turbine sound over the low rumbling was much more satisfying than the crude barking of domestic muscle cars. The tach needle jiggled at 1500 on a gauge that went to 10,000.

The test drive had been torturous. The salesman couldn't understand why Lorne didn't want to drive. They had motored onto the Fraser Highway to see what 0 to 60 felt like. His body was pushed back into the seat and in seconds they had punched through 180K.

Lorne had promised himself that he wouldn't drive the car until there was someone special in the passenger seat. On that happy day, he would take the ferry to Swartz Bay and drive that hairpin mess of a road between Nanaimo and Tofino, snapping the Porsche through turns so hard that the skin on their faces would be pulled from side to side, coming in so hot and fast that the brakes would smell. Love would flow and smiles would gleam like the snow on the mountain peaks, like sunlight off the hood of the car. The sexy passenger would rest his hand on Lorne's knee and this would make Lorne feel unexpectedly juvenile. It would be a Barbie moment, two guys having the most fun while others looked on and realized the most fun was being had.

Delaney's was packed but he only recognized other lonely men, deep into their books or glancing around, hungry. The thought of approaching anyone here made him cynical and tired. His list of former lovers would have made others envious in the eighties but changing times had redefined free sex as dangerous and pathetic. He wanted a loving man, not the kind of man who would come home with you one night and leave with your stereo while you slept, not a man who would leave you when he found out that despite your excellent physical condition you were actually forty-three years old, not a man who would have sex with everyone you knew at your gym including the staff, not the kind of man who would think love was tragic or dye his pubic hair purple because the others in his band did, not the kind of man who would talk about his wife and kids all the time and not understand why that hurt, not tri-sexuals, not men formerly known as women, not hustlers, drag-queens, dope-fiends, muscle freaks, no, not that, not any, not at all.

Just as Lorne realized that his latte was cold, someone bumped into him from behind. He turned to find that the bumper was beautiful: not the everyone-is-beautiful kind of beauty or a runner-up kind of inner beauty but a greedy, lusty, magazine kind of beauty. Brad apologized for his clumsiness and asked a question about the book Lorne was reading and soon they were talking about authors from England who deserved more attention and then Brad was sitting next to Lorne and brushing his knee against Lorne's leg and then they were walking on the beach and then Brad was making a joke about how the doors in the washrooms near the beach were cut to provide almost no privacy and all this was to prevent a few blow jobs and then Lorne was laughing at this, thinking of the shape of Brad's lips when he had said "blow job" and then, and then, and then Lorne was in love.

It didn't bother Lorne that Brad had almost nothing. Lorne's apartment was furnished and decorated exactly according to his taste and someone else's things would only interfere. When Brad explained how he lost almost all of his money on Bre-x, Lorne thought it was terribly romantic. Brad was good at attracting other people's money. It's what he did. It wouldn't be long before they'd be playing on a small mountain of cash.

They lived happily for two weeks. Then Brad started to attract some of Lorne's money. He said it was for operating expenses. He would need a little room to move because he had a big project in the works. "Room to move" was what he called it, insisting the money was an investment, not a loan. Lorne would thank him some day for the opportunity.

Lorne smiled when Brad modeled beautiful suits bought on Lorne's credit card but soon that smile started to fade. Brad and his outrageous telephone bills, calls to Singapore, Hong

Kong, Sydney. Brad and his room to move. And Brad was always too busy for Lorne's agenda. Sure, a road-trip to Tofino sounded great but for later on, after his "project" was up and running.

At parties he would approach Lorne's friends one by one, skillfully guiding them to a neglected part of the room to talk about limited time offers, ask them if they were interested in making a lot of money. It wouldn't be a matter of doubling your money—you'd get twenty, thirty, fifty times what you put in. Lorne was shocked at the serious interest Brad could generate from people who should have known better. Brad was a good-looking man with vision and energy and no one wanted to be left behind. Lorne learned to watch for the greedy, secretive look that overtook his friends as they leaned in closer to listen to Brad's quiet words. Later he would make calls to remind his friends that snake oil was not a good investment.

One day Lorne attended a conference on measles eradication in Victoria. He was embarrassed by how dull he found the whole thing and how distracted he was by the man in his life. He feared his lack of interest would be obvious to others so he made his face look contemplative and sensed where wise nods would be appropriate. At lunch, while everyone was sampling this or that recommended restaurant, he looked up a gym in the yellow pages and went for a workout.

At FitCo he asked a woman in the weight room for a spot on his third set of bench presses. It was Brenda's chest, back, and shoulders day as well, so they worked out together. They complained their way into a men-are-pigs conversation even though Lorne was not yet willing to call Brad a pig.

Brenda wanted to make him feel better relative to her horrible life so she told him about a beautiful man she had loved, who had taken all of her money, or rather, had accepted the money she gladly offered to him to support a project that was going to make them both rich. Attracting other people's money was what he did. When he heard that phrase, Lorne lost all of his strength causing 225 pounds to crash down on his sternum and stay there until Brenda helped him get the bar back up onto the cradle.

She didn't get the connection between her words and his sudden loss of power. She went on and on about how this user had worn her down. Every time they fought he would hug her to smother her fire, then smudge out her anger by rubbing the base of her spine. Soon after, he'd nudge her toward the bed and go down on her, doing that amazing thing with his tongue that had enslaved her and would keep him in her life long after they'd gone bad. He had these ways of getting what he wanted and a soft voice that made him hard to fight. And always, he would need more money, not a loan mind you, an investment. She hated being taken like that but couldn't stop herself. It wasn't a good example of feminist empowerment.

Lorne confronted Brad the next afternoon. Brenda, Brad said, was an experimental phase for him. They had met when he was recovering from an exciting but damaging romp with an abusive securities lawyer. She was there with kind words and a warm bed. It was something they just slipped into.

—I never said I was gay.

—Well, then you never told me you were bisexual.

—I never said I was bisexual.

—Then what are you, a very confused breeder?

Lorne disliked Brad's slippery nature. There were many advantages to being undefined, completely open to anything, and none of them were honourable. People who never committed to a position used their flexibility to get the most out of any situation without any sacrifice of their own. Lorne was angry and wanted to hang on to that anger, possibly work himself into a tantrum but Brad was soon behind him, lightly biting his shoulder, nudging Lorne toward the bedroom where Brad would go down on him, doing that amazing thing with his tongue that was beginning to enslave Lorne.

That weekend was a no-go for the Tofino trip. Brad was

very close to a breakthrough of massive proportions. He couldn't risk being out of town. Lorne, smoothed over from hours of sex, called Brenda to tell her about the "experiment" comment. That made her mad enough to release Chapter 2 of the Brad and Brenda saga. Brad had an interesting concept of fidelity. For him cheating was only cheating if you were caught. It was true that he had never lied about going to the baths, seeing dozens of other men and women. She had just assumed that he was monogamous. Brad liked to play with words. He liked logic when it suited him. He was careful with what he said because he had to be.

Brenda's bitterness boiled over every time she spoke with Lorne on the phone. She tried to be helpful and sympathetic, she tried to provide him with some kind of operations manual for Brad, but reliving the bad times brought out information that she knew would be damaging. She told Lorne about Active Pass Resort on Mayne Island. He took Monday off to check it out for himself. At the coffee shop near the ferry terminal the owner was the only one who would talk about Brad Newson. The patrons tried to set Lorne on fire with their hateful glares.

Four years ago Brad had arrived on the scene. He was a man with a plan and soon people were treating him like the Messiah. He came to "hire local people" to build a world-class resort. He hired them all right but he didn't pay them. The site was just up the road if Lorne wanted to look around for himself. Three kilometres inland, over a big stone gate, a large carved sign announced the Eagle Cove Resort. Someone had scribbled over the name with red spray paint. There were black marks at the base of the sign where someone had tried to burn it down. A wide, well-paved road that looked like the entrance to a new subdivision wound up into the woods for about two hundred metres. Lorne continued on a gravel road that turned into a muddy trail. The rental car laboured in deep ruts made by heavy equipment. Past a rusted-out bulldozer, a few tin-roof sheds and a pile of empty barrels lay Brad's world-class resort: a giant hole with a metre of water in it.

Library microfilm filled in the gaps with articles about an exciting young developer who had wowed the community and battled resistant bureaucrats and licensing bodies to ram through a project involving major multinational corporate partners. Everything looked great. And with the proposal generating great enthusiasm on the strength of Brad's presentation, each partner assumed the other guy was taking a close look at the numbers.

Brad sighed when Lorne brought it up. In business, he explained, many projects didn't turn out as planned. The majority of small businesses were failures. Speculative investments wiped out many people but it was the way the system functioned. You picked yourself up, dusted yourself off and started again.

What about your creditors though? That's what Lorne wanted to know. What would Barbie do with a life like his? Lorne felt certain she'd be too smart to end up with a bad date. At the first sign of trouble she'd be out the door and down the street, running reds in her Corvette to distance herself from her mistake. Why couldn't he internalize some of that Barbie wisdom? Present the best possible face at all times. Sweep through any room with the power of your perfection and always know where the party's at. He knew it was his fault that he attracted bad people, some flaw in him, some beacon on his head that attracted users and abusers. Barbie would never . . . Barbie would never.

Brenda's one-woman help line got a couple of calls a day from Lorne, who was trying to gauge the depths of Brad's psychopathy. During a long affirmation session in which Lorne was encouraged to stand his ground, insist on respect, not be swayed by the persuasive powers of his lover, Brenda let slip the name Denacran Construction.

Lorne soon realized that he could get more information

from Brenda if he gave false reports on Brad. He told her Brad had said she was a lousy lay, that she couldn't accessorize worth a damn and that she wasn't very cultured. That led to more information about Brad's Bre-X story, a story that went a little differently if you listened to his family, the ones who had put up the money for his gamble. It was only thirty thousand dollars but if he had sold at the top, as his family advised, he would have been a millionaire.

The nearest Denacran project was a building on 7th, not too far from the beach. Lorne didn't need the address. He just looked for a building covered by a huge plastic shroud. It was a common sight in Vancouver but he had never been that close to one of those money pits with its face ripped off and its rotting guts exposed.

He was shocked that the units were still occupied but it made sense—no one would be able to sell once the scaffolding went up and, having dumped their life savings into their new home, few would be able to afford alternate accommodations during the reconstruction.

Someone at work once told Lorne that living in a leaky condo was like going through an ugly, drawn-out divorce. First you'd notice little things like watermarks on the edge of the ceiling, a musty smell. At first mention of the "L" word you'd remember how those concerns had been brushed aside at the time of purchase. The buildings had been inspected and all the construction methods had been carefully regulated. That was enough to reassure most people when they signed. Leaky condos were someone else's problem. Then there'd be a wave of futile attempts to get some support from the crooks who made it. You'd discover how well the law protected them, how inspectors only checked electrical and plumbing and didn't even do a very good job of that. You'd be shuttered out from the real world by a plastic curtain, harassed by the noise of workmen who took their time and your money to repair the damage.

Lorne stopped under the streetlight and looked up to the

third floor. Someone was smoking on the balcony and there were faint noises of a party on the other side of the glass. The smoker flicked his butt down at Lorne and went back inside.

A woman passed Lorne and threaded between ladders and a wheelbarrow on her way to the front door.

—Excuse me. Do you live here?

She held the door open partway, looking back suspiciously at Lorne.

—Yes.

—Do you know anything about the company that built this place?

—Yes. They're not very good at what they do.

She was gone before Lorne could ask her anything else.

Brad accused Lorne of snooping and being judgmental. The buildings had been approved by municipal and provincial inspectors. There were affidavits to prove it. He had completely fulfilled his contractual obligations and if purchasers didn't read their purchase agreements then he couldn't be held responsible.

—I know, I know, Brad. You never lied.

The vague unease that Lorne felt was on the edge of articulation. Things were not likely to improve with time. The transforming power of love was a myth. There would be no conversion from psychopath to nice guy. Brad, the dealmaker, would always be bored by conventional business practice where customers got what they wanted or needed.

Lorne wasn't very good at endings. He replaced Brad's main door key with one of ten copies he had made of the old key. When Brad came home the next day his key didn't work, a garbage bag with his name on it sat on the steps, and Lorne wouldn't answer the intercom. Brad pounded on the door downstairs and all the residents, confident and secure in their mature relationships with reasonable and loving people, looked down at the entrance way where Brad was having an adolescent tantrum, screaming threats while he hurled clumps of mud from the flower bed at Lorne's window.

Some of the comments hurt Lorne as he sat in the chair next to the window with the blinds down. Breaking up was hard to do but mostly he was thinking of the wording of the ad he would place in the newspaper: 1999 Porsche Boxster. Mint condition. No mileage.

Genetic Attraction

TOM PASSES BY THE HOUSE, TAKING IN AS MUCH AS HE CAN IN his peripheral vision while avoiding a direct glance. He's early and this is his third time around the block. The house doesn't give away much: the grass is cut, there are no children's toys in the yard and no sign of a pet. It's a one-story with a covered garage, bland and inoffensive. On his fourth pass he veers up the driveway. The reflection in the window by the door looks pretty good, thanks to Muriel who had helped him pick out an outfit the night before. She had offered to come but that didn't seem right to Tom.

A girl about his age comes to the door. Before she can lead him to the living room he knows she has a problem with him. And the mother isn't even there. He knows he can just walk out if it gets too freaky. I'm so bored: that's Deanna's look, a pouty model or rock star whose apathy flows out like cool slime.

She thinks he's cute but badly dressed, a geek, a churchgoer, almost bad enough to cancel out his good looks. And he's timid, not really much of a man. An ugly grandfather clock measures the silence between them. She tells him that her mother—their mother—will be back soon.

He checks her out when she gets up to get him a glass of water. He wonders if she dresses this way all the time or if she had wanted to look good for his visit. She wears tight black pants, flared out slightly at the bottom, and shoes with ridiculously thick soles. The buttons on the front of her tight shirt are strained, making gaps that show her bra.

A car pulls into the driveway and Deanna lays down the rules in the time it takes her mother to gather her things, lock up the car and get to the front door.

—*Mother* is a generous title. Financial supporter might be a better label. I'm past the point of needing a mother anyway but the fact is that Tricia cannot be depended on for any kind of real support. Her life is real estate. She'll answer her cell even if she's sitting on the toilet. If someone calls during a meal she won't let the machine take it. If she doesn't answer the phone—and you'll hear this a lot—it might cost her thousands of dollars. It's fine to come here. It's fine to meet your birth mother but be prepared if you plan to become part of this family in any way. Be prepared to be slotted in efficiently, squeezed in between pressing engagements, postponed, put off, blown off and forgotten.

Tom thinks Tricia doesn't look like a mother as she stands in the doorway in a stylish suit, a wave of blonde hair coming down her sunglasses. She drops the grocery bags as if to further distance herself from domesticity. He's pleased with her lack of efficiency. She doesn't bustle by her two children to take the groceries directly to the kitchen, putting the frozen stuff away before it melts. She lets it sit in the foyer while she greets him with a handshake, then a hug.

Tricia realizes that she's been expecting some bitter attack, the heaping on of guilt. She doesn't feel defensive because the tall, shy man leaning against the wall with his hands in his pockets does not seem angry. His eyes are wide for everything they see. Scrutiny without the judgement, one of his father's strengths.

Deanna notices the thousand-dollar suit right away, and the new hair. Both of them seem desperate to make a good impression, to like and be liked. It's embarrassing, almost sickening to watch them, nervous and giddy, like two kids on a first date. It's a phase, she wants to tell them, you'll get over it.

After months of severe restrictions Deanna now has total social freedom. It should make her happier than it does. The curfews, the constant monitoring, even the occasional intercepted phone call had been intended to keep Deanna from hanging around stoners, snowboard freaks, anyone who could drag her grades down, anyone who was fun and had a life. Since Tom's first visit Deanna's been staying out later and later with no complaint from Tricia. When she came in at 6:30 AM, her mother asked if she had been at a sleepover or something. Or something. Deanna could be freebasing coke, dating a biker gang or raising llamas in her bedroom and Tricia might not even notice.

Tricia is into Tom. They sit close together on the couch and look at photo albums. They drink tea, laugh at each other's stories and swap CDs, now that Tricia's musical taste is fifteen years younger. Deanna is tired of seeing them together, coming out of her room only to scavenge for food and use the bathroom.

Tom doesn't want to ruin his fun by thinking about it too much but he's thrilled to have found his mother. He visits almost every day. Tricia is about a hundred years younger than his fake mother, likes the music he plays for her, and does not laugh at his claim that *Terminator 2* is the greatest action film ever made. He talks to her as he would talk to a friend.

On the way back from the bathroom Tricia stares at the No

Trespassing sign on Deanna's door, a two-year-old, semi-serious warning to respect Deanna's privacy. If the guardedness and distancing is a phase, it's been a long one. Once Deanna's deep into one of her moods, trying to talk about it just makes it worse. Better to ignore it. The dirty truth is that Tricia is relieved when her daughter leaves at night. After the front door slams the house seems to settle almost immediately.

Tom gets up to leave around 11:00 PM and gives Tricia a big hug at the door. She loves this about him, the easy physical affection. Down the hallway a door closes and Deanna's stereo goes on. They stand in the dark foyer with yellow light from a street lamp making a shadow of their fused form.

He gets a hard-on while thinking about how embarrassing it would be to get a hard-on. It's slow at first, then urgent, worming its way under the top elastic of his underwear. He's not concerned. It doesn't necessarily mean anything. Since he was thirteen his hard-ons have been triggered by thoughts of sex, as well as satin boxer shorts, the name Anastasia, a warm wind out of the southwest, saunas, lingering soapings in the shower, sitting on an unbalanced washing machine, and riding at the back of the bus.

She feels his heart pounding before he moves away and assumes he must be overcome with the emotion, the sudden power of this reunion, the relief of being accepted.

Muriel feels an icy fist squeezing her gut. Jealousy is a sin. She'd rather be happy for Tom and his enthusiasm for his birth mother. She hopes to feel the correct emotions soon. He missed church on Sunday. Friends at Bible study asked about him. He missed youth group on Wednesday. She only has snippets of his voice on her answering machine from two weeks ago when things were normal, when he was fully her man.

Games Night was unbearable without him. Couples paired off around the fireplace to give each other massages while she filled up on popcorn twists at the unlucky end of the basement, playing a game called Sorry with the unattached and unloved. Between throws of the die she remembered the weight of his hands on her, the way they would plane from her lower back to her shoulders. On the return his fingers would come down the sides of her body, his fingertips just brushing past her breasts.

She knows his sudden interest in family is a good sign of his future father potential but she misses his hands, his insistent body pressed against hers. She will continue to give up tiny plots of her territory as they kiss for hours in his basement but they will still be virgins on their wedding night. She won't end up like those sluts at school, getting pregnant, jumping from bed to bed, getting who knows what kinds of diseases.

On Friday the youth group's going bowling. He'll probably miss that too.

Tricia is surprised by Tom's techniques. She has a sore neck and a headache but he soothes both with his skilled touch. She tells him about the couple from Malaysia who didn't speak any English, the translator who didn't seem to translate everything she was saying, comments he made to the clients that made them look at her and laugh. The gentle circles Tom makes with his fingers make her run out of words in the middle of a sentence.

The bed is a better place to receive a massage and she is, after all, exhausted from work. It's hard for him to really get at her back from the side. Straddling her allows better access. It's much easier with her blouse off and the bra strap undone. Tricia doesn't really think before she asks if he'd like to do her front.

Tricia encourages Tom to call her by her first name now, not that it's ever been an issue. Tom has been very careful not to say mom or mother, to avoid the presumption. She runs into a friend at the mall. She introduces Tom and does not explain anything. A superficial conversation follows, the friend straining to make sense of it, put it into context.

When Deanna comes home early from school, Tricia's legs clamp down on Tom's head to stop his movement. Her heart is pounding as she waits for the sound of Deanna's bedroom door closing. They lie there gripping each other until they hear her radio. The house is too risky.

Deanna hasn't actually seen her mother for a few weeks now. Sometimes Deanna hears her in the kitchen or in the bathroom, taking a shower. Tricia has taken to communicating with her daughter by writing notes. Here's twenty bucks if you feel like ordering pizza. Really busy with work. Sorry. Love you, Mom. Deanna suspects Tricia doesn't realize how many times she has done this in the last week.

Do you want to come with me? That's how it starts, the first time she takes him to a showing. The client is polite to Tom when introduced but there's that puzzled look again. The three of them walk through the high-rise condo. High ceilings. A great view of Central Park. Five appliances included. Hardwood.

Tricia sees the client out, shutting the door behind him and Tom is instantly behind her, working off her skirt. With her palms flat against the door she turns her head to find his mouth. The buckle from his belt knocks against the floor. Without fear of being heard by her daughter, she cries out, surprising them both.

From then on, she brings a blanket to lay over the owners' bedding or floor or table.

—Is this yours? I found it in the back seat of the car.

Deanna shows Tricia the used condom she holds between the thumb and forefinger of her rubber-gloved hand.

—Maybe one of your boyfriends left it there.

—This is ribbed. I never used ribbed. Do you know how I found it? It was stuck to my friend's shoe. I had to tell her it was mine because I didn't want her to know that my mother's a slut who likes to fuck her own son. That's right, I know all about it. How stupid do you think I am?

Tricia backs away, furious, red-faced and powerless.

Muriel can't understand God's plan for her life. She found someone she liked, she fell in love with him, she planned to marry him, and then he broke up with her by leaving a message on her answering machine. Her little brother, the first to hear it, plays it back many times for the benefit of the rest of the family, laughing as he does because even he knows how tacky it is despite the fact that he's in grade six and has never been on a date.

Tom's voice on the machine sounds like he's being held hostage. That woman has done something to him. Perhaps she's convinced him that Muriel isn't good enough for him, that he could do better.

She goes to Tom's house to search for a non-existent earring. He probably hasn't told his parents about the breakup yet. She had a number of different stories prepared, depending on what they knew, but they had been friendly and open when she called. Searching through his things for that woman's address is wrong but she has to protect him. Small sins to prevent greater evil.

Muriel's ready to fight for what's hers. If Tom wants her out of his life for good then he'll have to say so face to face. She won't be dumped just because some woman she's never met thinks that she's not good enough for him. It's hard to "Let Go and Let God" when it's something you can't be without.

At the door of Tricia's house Muriel announces herself as Tom's girlfriend. Deanna smiles.

—Come on in. We have a lot to talk about.

Only Tricia knows it's their last time together. On the bed in a property on Sussex, Tom is going on about plans for the future, how they could move to the States or somewhere in Canada where no one knew them. She could sell real estate anywhere, right? It's possible. And why is she so sad?

—They know.

—Who knows?

—My daughter. Your girlfriend.

—She's not my girlfriend. I broke up with her.

—She'll take you back. She told me she would.

—But I don't want her.

—Listen Tom, the two of them are going to make our lives hell if we don't end this. They'll ruin my career and they'll destroy your reputation.

—I thought you said you didn't care what other people thought.

—I didn't mean my own daughter.

She tells him that he doesn't really want this. Some things you can't have. What would he tell his friends and family? Why did he refuse to see it for what it was? The relationship was doomed from the start. That's what made the whole thing so intense. But secrecy was a power that turned into a weakness. She thought he knew it would go like this. One of them had to do something.

He looks like he's trying to squirm out of this, away from her words. She never would have guessed that Tom was this immature, stomping around the room, pulling at his hair. It's like being back in high school. He's acting like a teenager. She wonders for a moment if it's all an act. Her last breakup had all the passion of someone switching mutual funds.

In her fantasy breakup she would have arranged something smooth but caring. He would, of course, realize that she was right, the relationship could not go on. They would spend their final moments in a sad loving embrace. His last kiss would linger at her neck.

Tricia waits for Tom to turn over the key. Tom pleads while she gets dressed. It takes him forever to work her key off his ring. Time slows down. He finally offers it to her in his palm and when she reaches for it he grabs her hand. When she twists out of his grip he pounds the wall with his fist, creating a small crater in the drywall. Now she'll have to call a repairman before she shows the place again. Hopefully he won't wreck anything else.

She wishes he'd stop pacing the room in his shorts, crying like a baby in diapers. Leaving him the second time is just as hard.

Safe Places on Earth

"No mercy without imagination"
—Somebody

I'VE BEEN FROM COAST TO COAST, CROSSING BORDERS IN TRUCKS or rattling motorhomes. I have stolen lunch money, firearms, and clothes from a laundromat dryer. Once I rolled a paperboy. I have been kicked in the head by a hooker I tried to rob in Denver. I lay in the dirt while she squatted over me and washed my cuts with her piss, stuffing a dirty American twenty in my mouth. I am the wrong kind of famous in Montana and Nova Scotia.

My life is rich and meaningless.

Rivers, MB

Combine lights, seen from the bus window, sweep along the dry prairie stubble, and below it, in the darkness, the wide mouth pulls in its straight flat tongue of wheat.

Coming into Rivers in perfect time, the tail end of summer, harvest time, with gears spinning in their hot grease all day, slowing only when the women come in pickups to bring hot meals in tin-foil, their asses filling the grooves of the tires.

Stepping off the bus into the dusty heat, walking along the bridge over the creek, up the hill, down the gravel lane between the windbreak where the dogs begin to bark and run towards me.

A yard light switches on, another in the kitchen, throwing a square of light onto the yard. Standing on the front steps, hoping the Dycks will remember me from three summers ago.

Mrs. Dyck silent behind the screen door in a shadow while she puts her glasses on. Pushing the door towards me and pulling me into the parallel dimension of the Rural Manitoba Farmhouse, unchanged from one year to the next, Bible verses hanging from small plaques over the kitchen table, butterfly fridge magnets holding up the shopping list, and the smells of summer sausage, *Zwieback* and *Rollkuchen*.

Strangers

There are three types of strangers: the complete stranger, the perfect stranger and the total stranger. I am all of these.

The complete stranger has nothing and that is exactly what he needs. He has appeared and will appear in the future as someone who belongs exactly where he is at any given time. You don't look twice at his face because he has always been there and when he leaves you will not notice. When he is gone you will not remember. The perfect stranger is almost always grey and when he is not grey he is beige. These are the primary colours of the man-made world in which he can easily hide. In order to hide from you, he would sit right next to you while grey thoughts looped in his brain, as he sat with grey posture and matched the grey faces of those around him. The total stranger is the sum of the parts of his life.

Rivers, MB

The Dycks had enough help for harvest that first summer but they let me do odd jobs like bringing meals to the men or painting fence posts. I spent time around the house, snooping through their things. In the sewing room, on the top shelf, I found back issues of the *Mennonite Reporter* from '72 on. There were Mennos everywhere from Skookumchuck to Madagascar. I had discovered a network of gullible do-gooder pacifists ready to be exploited. The Dycks were delighted with my interest in the Mennonite church.

When I had enough information, I began writing reference letters for myself. I started with names:

Peter Dyck
Irene Friesen
Agnes Paetkau
Bernie Wiens
Henry Loewen
John Remple
Elmwood Mennonite Church
"Sing to the Lord" Mennonite Choir

Dear Bernie (pastor of target church):

You probably don't remember me but we met at the '82 General Conference in Wichita, Kansas (lie) and participated in a discussion group on "The Healing Power of Christ" (lie). I have fond memories of our fellowship and sharing (big lie).

I am writing this letter to introduce you to John Remple, a dedicated member of our congregation who has decided to move to Calgary in order to be closer to his sister who is ill (lies, lies, lies).

John has just been through a troubling time (no

job, no money, no future) and would appreciate your support (how about a place to stay?)

Many Conference members here have spoken of your generosity and unfailing stewardship (meaningless Christian buzzword that will induce guilt if John (me) does not receive assistance).

I'm sure John will benefit greatly from your guidance (implied request and assumption that Bernie will help).

Yours sincerely (tee hee),

Henry Loewen
Elmwood Mennonite Church

Language
The alphabet is my best weapon.
It's all there.

abcdefghijklmnopqrstuvwxyz

▲

That's all you need
to slip through bars
or start a holy war.

Mennonite Ideology

Mennonites believe in God. I believe in Mennonites, but through my reading I have come to a disturbing revelation: modern Mennonite faith is based on prudence. The original movement was not. Early converts ran from disgruntled clergy who wanted to stretch them on racks, castrate them with white-hot pincers and scrape out their eyes with wire brushes.

It has become a comfortable religion. Those who met in caves and shared the dangerous new words would be disappointed to find their pale followers clinging to ancient ideals that have become easy to hold, even fashionable.

I doubt that you could sell the religion in its original form. Believe this, even though they might torture you. Say this, even though you might die. Untested faith leaves modern followers spiritually fat.

Drowning

How could you call it murder? I was holding his head. Underwater. And I kept holding it and I remember it was very hot for early morning and the water was just over my waist in the murky muddy Assiniboine so that I couldn't see him beneath the surface.

How long did I hold him after he had stopped thrashing? Half an hour or an hour? How could it have been anything but peaceful, letting go, letting him drift free of my hands, his hair through my fingers?

Camp

The camp is dark except for one light at the main centre. It's a Mennonite camp which means that I must stay in the empty counsellors' quarters till midnight, then stumble to her mobile without a flashlight and hiss under her window screen.

In the morning I watch from the arena fence as she drives in horses from pasture, her chin down slightly, warmed by the rough Carhartt, small branches slapping her chinks. She dismounts the horse named 3-10 and begins to cut away horses for the first ride of the day.

An old canner named May, who has become fond of me over the last few days, wanders over to me. Flies eat her eye sand and I can tell by the lazy way she blinks that she's tired. She moves away when Michelle comes to get her for the ride but Michelle keeps walking after her, walking, as I witness her patience and love her for it, walking.

Things I miss

1.) My name
2.) The luxury of answering the door
3.) The luxury of answering the phone
4.) The luxury of arousing suspicion
5.) The luxury of telling the truth
6.) The exotic and comforting mediocrity of beef stroganoff, venetian blinds and a full bag of grass clippings by the curb.
7.) Credit cards

Fisherman's Wharf

Which one was it? Rows and rows of dumpy plywood shacks that floated. She slowed in the middle of Dock "C" in front of the smallest one, painted like a zebra. Her home was refreshing or insane, just like the occupant, and as we stepped on and sent a set of oily ring waves across

Fisherman's Wharf, I thought of our position on the water, floating on top of something huge, like a water bug must feel on a lake, buoyed by tension only, and that solid land was not really solid, but rather a large floating raft constantly moving, and things were more fragile and temporary than they seemed. I had all those thoughts waiting for Ms. Klassen to unlock the hatch and when she finally did I grabbed her ass with both hands as she bent over to step in and I forgot about my lake-bug existence.

Britannia Yacht Club

There's a place where you can go to stand and wait as they pass in their boats. And if you've had a chance to shave and comb your hair and are wearing clothes that aren't obviously dirty you might be asked to crew. A woman might come over while her boat is being refuelled and invite you on board.

And moments later you're wrapping rope around a capstan and telling ferocious lies, inventing new extended families and an intricate personal history.

The captain decides to give up the race you have entered. Cut-throat crazy rich people slice past on either side as the helmsman sets a course for the islands where you drop anchor.

Several wine bottles later, you fling the bones of the BBQ chicken overboard and loll about in your fattened state. The anchor is pulled, the sun is setting, a course is set and the boat is moving slowly, one sail only.

Definitions

Criminal—Not in any way resembling a human. No one you might know or would have raised.

Hardened criminal—Label used to justify any punishment.

Cold-blooded murder—The opposite of hot-blooded murder. Severity of punishment according to temperature of blood. Crime done under influence of childish fit deemed to be less serious regardless of end result. The incident in Billings was unavoidable. The temperature of my blood was ninety-eight point six degrees.

Correctional institute—The cage, prison, jail, the bighouse, the can, the slammer, joint, summer camp, headwaters of Shit Creek, where criminals (see def'n) go to get hardened, fun house, repentance factory, the zoo, hell's waiting room, not a deterrent, not a cure, society's bottom drawer.

Safe places on earth—The only safe place on earth is a coffin.

Regina, SK

I am dining with the parents of the singer I fucked last night. The roast beef is dry but the meal is saved by a sharp chutney and perfectly roasted carrots. The struggle-with-faith act I used on the girl has similar success with the arrogant ABS, RSP, GIC, PhD father, who assures me that despite his obvious and overwhelming success as a human, he too had once doubted the Mennonite faith.

He is preaching about what the scripture clearly tells us while I am thinking about the girl who sits across from me, trying to smell her no-nonsense Christian-white panties, her soap, the excessive baby powder she puffs up into her armpits every morning.

This act is the strongest of my Christian series personas. Being lost invites the target Christian to lead, something they cannot resist. With women it brings out a mothering instinct, especially in those who are in desperate need of mothering themselves.

And so, the concert last night, a Mennonite choir, the scanning of rows of women, their lips making openings of various shapes and sizes, a vulnerable face, a game of eye tag setting us on tracks that will join, compliments after the concert, her suggestion to join the group for coffee, staying at the restaurant until all the others had left, my hint about my troubled life, my dilemma, my weakness feeding her strength, her chance to be her own mother and mother herself, my polite and timid manner and the way I stand next to her car in the parking lot, looking like I don't know where I should or could go next, that practiced look of no direction, lamb before slaughter, innocent, a look that guarantees access to whatever a victim can offer: a ride, a cup of herbal tea, a comforting hand on the shoulder, pity for my well-timed tears, a comforting hand on the breast, displaced stuffed animals and thick comforters, etc.

I cannot help but be impressed by the skills I have developed. My head nods, my pupils face Our Father, my nose seeks traces of a woman while I appraise the potential postfence value of the stereo in the living room, Yamaha, I think, flirting with me, its decibel band flashing an invitation.

The future

when I reach sixty
I will no longer be able
to deny anything

fingering the holes in my heart
standing with my heart in my hands
fingering the holes and tears

I will be
barefoot on the concrete
standing on every corner at once

Stepping out of Winter, out of Dreams

HOW IT GOT THIS BAD, I DON'T KNOW. THE APARTMENT IS LIKE an opium den without the smoke, no one shuts their door anymore, no one seems to care.

In stages, Winnipeg has cut us off from the outside world. Two weeks ago he stopped answering the phone. Then the answering machine was switched off, along with the ringer. Finally, he disconnected the system and threw the tape in the garbage. I've listened to it so I know it's urgent that Winnipeg call Donna, that Eu Jin know why Singapore missed his lab, and that Petro needs his calculator back. If anyone came to visit they would be able to tell that something is wrong, but no one visits.

The days are short, warped into a feeble pale space. And despite my new winter parka that everyone insisted I must have, winter in Canada is colder than I could have imagined. Now I see hell as a cold place with ice caves, no sunshine, icicles hanging from everything.

At 4:30 the sun fills a crack between cloud and horizon. I get up and eat breakfast in the orange light, grateful for a few minutes of sun. Singapore comes to the table with hair uniquely styled by an afternoon of rough sleep. Winnipeg joins us as the sun disappears. He watches snow fall on the cemetery six floors down. Inside, we suffer in warm dry air heated to imitate Singapore's tropical home. Outside, snowflakes cover the names of the dead, the lucky ones, those who have left us behind to struggle with the elements.

I like to complain to Winnipeg just to piss him off. I tell him Canada sucks. Teasing him is easier than doing my work. It helps me forget that my friends are studying hard right now and will continue to study long after I have fallen asleep. It gets dark. I begin my review of how electric flux relates to Gauss's Law and nonconducting infinite plates with a surface change and coaxial cables:

HONG KONG'S DREAMING

I am in the BMW showroom. All around me, the latest offerings from Germany. Mother holds the tarp that covers my gift. As my friends surround me I can see their jealousy. Most of them are still taking the bus or driving Chevettes and Pintos.

Anna-Lyn is smiling and holding my hand. Could it be a 735i? Maybe an M1 shipped over from Europe and modified for North American roads. My smiling mother tugs off the tarp to reveal a brand new...Honda Civic. Anna-Lyn's hand still clings. It's a brand new Civic. White. With no extras.

One friend starts to laugh, then others, cruelly pointing at my new Honda Civic white with no extras. Anna-Lyn is blushing and squirming to get away from me, my disgrace.

I cry into my hands and when I take them away my eyebrows stick to my fingers. I try to stick them back on my face but then my eyelashes come off as well. Each time I try to stick something back, more parts come off until my cheeks are bloody and raw, my tongue, my skin, rubbery and hot.

dr is dq F= pdV = p4 r dr

Eu Jin probably memorized this chapter weeks ago. I don't think he ever sleeps, just plows ahead, red-eyed, determined, superior. I forget to blink. My eyes dry out. My brain demonstrates a preference for rumination over formula memorization. The rigid logic of physics provides little protection against the absurdity of my existence here.

My father paid the government a quarter million to get us here so I could study a language I'll never use while Iranian factions fight holy wars in the University Centre cafeteria on "International Day," zealots of one kind or another fire random shots at buildings from cars.

The theme from *The Golden Girls* rips through my soft dreams. I've been sleeping for an hour and a half with my face in my textbook. As part of our ritual Winnipeg calls me an asshole and tells me to get to work.

He likes to think he's a writer. He sits in front of the television with a note pad and a pen and usually manages to produce one or two really interesting doodles. On less productive days the page remains blank and he goes to bed with angry red eyes. I once told him, if you want to be a writer you're going to have to write something. We covered the hole he punched in the wall with a calender of great Canadian landscapes. I no longer try to remove his delusions. Last week he punctuated his rebuttal by chopping my calculus text in half with a #1 cleaver.

He distracts me when he could be doing something more productive like jerking off. I retaliate with subtle attacks on his language. I like to come home from the bar and tell Winnipeg that there were a lot of horny womans out that night. Sometimes I tell him I have to go downstairs to the laundry room to wash my clothings.

When Hong Kong walks in with his phone we anticipate a repeat of last night's argument with his mother, pleading for money, threatening not to come home for the summer if his

SINGAPORE'S DREAMING

Thais are the best killers in the world.
Chinese, Malaysians and the Japanese join
them, tailing me through the dockyards,
through the market, as I run. They are patient
because they know I will soon be out of breath.
I glance back to catch the flash of light off a
spinning weapon. The Thais approach
unarmed. I begin to understand inevitability.

***

I sit in front of the doctor's desk and try not
to shrink from his cruel eyes. I explain to him
that my palms get sweaty, I should be exempt
from practise. He tells me to make a tight fist. I
do, trying to squeeze sweat from my pores. I
open my hands for examination. The doctor is
unconvinced. I am sent out to the field with my
pail of grenades.

To throw it, I bring it over my heart, cold
metal nested between my breasts, then to my
lips to kiss the rough grip before throwing it as
hard as I can. The grenade goes straight up and
falls at my feet. I throw it again but the same
thing happens. I throw it again. I throw it
again. And again.

needs aren't met.
Basic student transportation must take
the form of a BMW
325i. His mother
has countered with
offers of a Honda
Civic but Hong
Kong is unimpressed. His parents
remind him that he
has gone through
10K of spending
money in four
months. For the
first time they seem
reluctant to send
more. He slams his
cellular down on
the table, glowing
buttons flicker from
the shock.

The ultra-violence of a Chinese
gangster video matches his mood. After a few thousand
rounds have been exchanged he starts talking to me in the
sudden friendly tone of a user. I know before he asks that his
problem is with the last few pages of chapter eight. He has
probably tried his friends, although many of them don't
understand either and are quite willing to confuse him further
rather than admit their own ignorance. Like most of the people I know from Hong Kong, I don't like him very much.
He'll use me but he doesn't respect me because I'm Korean.
Instead of helping him I say I don't understand that part.
Thankfully, there's not much he can say to that. He leaves

after I prove useless to him. I won't be able to study anymore tonight so I head to my room.

Singapore's light is still on. I knock quietly and open the door. He sleeps on a mat on the floor. The arrangement of his things suggests that he is preparing for hibernation, as if somewhere there are stores of nuts and berries, enough to last through winter. The windowless room feels like a burrow, a suitable place to wallow in words, equations and formulas. Piles of crumpled sheets and dirty clothing make a comfortable nest. A stack of textbooks keeps him reading continuously, no need to come out.

KOREA'S DREAMING

In the morning I arrive at Brooks Hall to write my final exam. It's empty. The exam is due to start in five minutes but there is no one there. Despite the fact that I have triple checked the time and location, I take another look at the notice. It says the exam is being held at Mon Petit on the other side of campus. I run as fast as I can into the building, down the hall. I can see my friends cheering for me but before I arrive the professor walks up to the entrance and locks the doors. I pound on them but no one lets me in.

I wait outside for three hours for the sound of the lock opening, the emergence of my classmates, joking and laughing, wearing expensive clothing and jewelry.

Singapore is wandering again. I can tell from my room by the sound of his fingers tracing the walls, the small tender bumps as he bumbles his way down the hall and into the living room. Sometimes he will get caught in a corner and stand there with his forehead leaning against it, like a battery-powered toy that has picked a bad direction.

He's more ambitious in his sleep than in any other state. I say this because he doesn't just walk around, he does *kata*. Somehow aware of the spatial limitations of the room, he manages to do karate forms without breaking a thing.

He goes back to bed and sleeps peacefully until 4:00 when his dreamtime ravings wake me. There is short choppy yelling, then silence. A few moments later I hear him slamming drawers and throwing down hangers. He is on his way out when I intercept him in the hallway.

—What are you doing?

—I'm getting out of here.

—Are we too noisy? Can't you sleep?

—Sleep is all that I can do here. My room has no windows. I never know when to get up. I've been having awful dreams and lately I've been having everyone else's awful dreams. I'm leaving.

—Where will you go?

—U of O res. Eu Jin says his roommate is never there so I can sleep in his bunk.

—You haven't finished.

—What do you mean?

—You're part of what's happening.

Singapore stays, pacified by one of his own classic meals that I've learned to prepare: fried spam strips and Ichiban noodles.

Winnipeg begins to record

WINNIPEG'S DREAMING

I am looking at a woman or I am a woman. A man is guiding me through the Gidian Desert. He walks ahead of me, dismantling bombs and booby-traps. A bomb blows off his hand. He sits me down in the sand and spends two days telling me everything he knows about defusing explosives. He goes ahead after this and tries to defuse a bomb with his wrong hand. It explodes and kills him.

dream confessions and every scrap of information, every word that strays into his senses. He flips from channel to channel, collecting five-word snippets, catching breakfast conversation about soggy cornflakes. He spends time searching Singapore's textbook for pretty words, quizzing Singapore as he flips through it.

Everyone has become self-conscious about what they say. I

find myself attempting to communicate in words and phrases that may have some literary value.

Yesterday Winnipeg tried to record a Chinese phone call as Hong Kong's mother told him she didn't care if he came home, he wasn't getting any more money. Hong Kong slammed the phone down on the table and did a furious little dance that we couldn't help giggling about. He called her a bitch, he called her a whore, he called her the stinking shit of a sewer rat. He has decided to drop out of school, a move that is bound to be popular with the academic authorities who put him on probation three months ago. Next week he is going for an interview at McDonald's, expecting to be hired as a manager.

Winnipeg is mapping the progression of dreams. In his transcripts it is noted that Hong Kong is beginning to dream more about his mother. He is dining in a fancy restaurant with his girlfriend when his mother smashes through the roof with a huge rubbery arm and pulls Hong Kong up through the hole and throws him into a back alley where there are bums eating dog food out of cans. Little has changed with Singapore's dreams, except now killers from all over the world are carrying cleavers and chasing him in black BMWs. Korea dreamed that he was in grade school again. The children were chopping off their hands by opening desk tops and then slamming them on their tender wrists.

I am only mildly curious when I go to answer a knock at the door at 1:00 expecting some drunk from the party next door in need of ice, or Eu Jin seeking refuge from his noisy Res.

Instead, a beautiful woman with too much perfume on stares at me from across the threshold, then pushes past me. She sets up a cheap little radio, lays down a blanket in front of the TV and takes off her coat. When music starts the others peek out of their holes, gather around the woman in stiletto heels. Flirting with me, circling me, she drops the tasselled outfit, revealing a skimpy bra, then nothing but angry, sharp bikini lines.

—Happy Birthday, Rick, she says to me, giving me a naughty smile.

I am unable to tell her my birthday is in April, my name is not Rick. The four of us stand silently, trusting that the woman will know how to end what she has started. It may be the polite yet shocked faces or the absence of hooting and howling but eventually she begins to suspect that something is wrong. She digs the order slip out of her bag. She becomes scared and defensive, demanding that one of us be Rick, celebrating his thirtieth. She almost leaves without her radio, hiding from us the body she had so enthusiastically displayed. I turn to Winnipeg.

—Now you have something to write about.

—What would I write? A stripper had the wrong apartment number? Some story.

—You could describe her. Us. The details.

—Describe what?

—Everything. Record everything and take out the crap later.

Hong Kong, unable to sleep after the stripper, is playing ping-pong off the window. I'm watching videos as the ball flies past me. It is 3:32. Elsewhere in the apartment, the sounds of industry, or at least crumpling paper.

The ping-pong ball is annoying for more than the obvious reasons. It hits against glass and glass is more cruel than a prison wall. I catch the ball and stomp on it with my heel.

I open the window as far as it will go and suck in fresh air. By the reflection, I see a resigned Hong Kong looking for another ball.

Pulling against the hallway door, I feel the strong suction as the seal is cracked. Giant vents are dragging fresh air from the open window into the heart of the building.

The feel of the carpet on my bare feet compels me to cart-wheel down the hallway to our neighbour's door. My foot just misses the fire alarm.

The important red handle waits for a case of emergency. I study it closely, lick the cold glass tube. It resists the tender wet pressing of my tongue. Caressing the handle, my fingers pass my pulse into metal, under the explosive bell.

Our lives are in a state of emergency and the seconds are precious. We choose to ignore this as I choose to ignore the siren outside, getting louder as it nears our building, fading as it passes.

I could pull the handle but I know that not all calls for help are answered. If I cannot explain our emergency, we will be ignored. Not everyone can be helped.

I know that I've come to the end of something with my latest dream but I don't know what to do about it. It is dark. Our building has no walls, making it look like a giant stack of shelves. We are lined up side by side with our toes on the edge of the floor. The cemetery stretches on for as far as I can see. There are no lights. Directly below us there are four open graves that are partially filled with snow. Hong Kong dives first, straight and rigid, end over end and screaming, not from fear but to release the pain he's been carrying. We see a puff of snow as the body hits the grave. The others follow. I am the last one to jump. When I do, I float slowly to the ground. I think I hear something from one of the graves. I can hear it if I stand still. Singapore, I think. I want him to give me his hand so I can pull him out. I want him to keep calling to help me find him.

Singapore is yelling in his bedroom. He doesn't respond at all to the usual poking and light face slapping. Winnipeg grabs his legs while I grab his arms, pulling him straight, out of the fetal curl. He starts to thrash about with his eyes still closed. Winnipeg is knocked back over a pile of books.

Hong Kong, who has been watching from the doorway, turns off the light and closes the door. We can hear his laughter from outside the room. Someone is following the wall to get to the door. That sounds stops and then I hear a struggle. I move toward it and grab a limb. I don't know who I'm holding but my goal is restraint. I hope it's Singapore I'm sitting on. If not, he may be about to smash my head in with a three-hole punch. I'm hanging on to sweaty dark flesh in a windowless room and very much wanting this to be over.

Winnipeg finds the light. He is whimpering from the pain of his bloody nose. He helps me haul the squirming fighter into the bathtub, roughly pressing the shower-head into Singapore's face.

Dazed and bruised, Singapore insists on taking us out to the twenty-four-hour Waffle House. It sounds bizarre, like robbing a 7-11 or having breakfast on the ice in the middle of the Ottawa River but it seems inevitable. Before we leave I turn on everything, every light, every radio, the TV. The phone rings as soon as I plug it in but no one moves to answer it. Clearing out bad air takes strength, light and noise. I march around, banging a serving spoon against a fry-pan. Being the last one out, I leave the door fully open.

We trudge through thick snowfall in a slight breeze and I think absently how each day the light stays two minutes longer. Singapore gives me a funny look. Maybe he thinks I saved him through blood and force and cold water, saved him from being drugged on his own dreams, slipping between this world and the other.

We have worked our way past the middle of winter, forward and upward. The snow crews scrape snow off the street and spread salt. The Waffle House is almost within reach, its large yellow sign standing out like a revelation.

What Colour Is Your Electric Chair?

THE FLIGHT FROM VANCOUVER DRAINED ME SO BADLY THAT I fell asleep in the limo that picked me up at the airport. I had a dream about riding backwards on a roller coaster a thousand feet above the ocean. When the driver woke me I was completely disoriented and remained so even as he led me to my room and closed the door behind me. In the bathroom I noticed that my makeup was smudged and my hair was a mess. It was not until I had checked the hotel stationery that I was convinced I was in Niagara Falls.

This is the last day of testing and I'm thinking of pulling out. I'm lying on the bed at 3:00 AM, waiting for Raymond, who will provide even more graceful ways to fail. The interviews are like bad blind dates.

Yesterday, during our out-and-about interview on the Stanley Park sea wall, I tried again to get more information out of Raymond.

—I'm not going any farther with this until you tell me what position I'm applying for.

—Your sponsor thinks you have excellent potential for a

number of positions. Based on that, you were selected for the interview process.

—Who is my sponsor?

—Someone you know.

—Could you be more specific?

—Your sponsor is someone you've been close to for years, someone who knows you very well.

—Could you be more specific?

—No. Oh, and if you're thinking of pulling out—that's pretty common at this point—your sponsor wants me to tell you that it's worth it. You shouldn't pass on the opportunity.

—What opportunity?

—Employment with Ulford.

—God, you people are maddening!

I call Vancouver and wake up my boyfriend to check up on things. Darrell goes right at it again, about my interview process, how strange it is, how the men who had called for me last month seemed like freaks. Since we last talked he's done some checking: there is no Ulford Co. registered in British Columbia or anywhere else. There are no references to Ulford Co. on the Internet. The reference desk at the VPL has nothing on Ulford Co. Maybe I had the name wrong. He drones on and for once I'm intensely grateful for the mundane familiarity of his voice.

TELL ME ABOUT YOURSELF.

On Tuesday, I was in Calgary with the very serious Mark. First thing, he questioned my commitment. If I were really serious about this process I would get to appointments on time. Maybe, as a woman, I found it difficult to get anywhere on time. Was that my problem? A sale I saw on the way here that I couldn't pass up? Was that it? He asked about relocation, plane crashes, and made me sit through a long rant about the Exocet missile while we drove to the Calgary General Hospital. A number of times during the rant he claimed to be a "people person." When I was sure that he had finished, I attempted small talk.

—That doesn't look like a regular cell phone.

—It isn't.

Mark's instructions were in tiny red letters on a piece of yellow paper. I went to the fourth floor and avoided the front desk when I stepped off the elevator. I found Room E27, went in and closed the door. There was only a small light on near the bed. The old man seemed to be in pain but he was too weak to make much noise about it. He wanted me to give him something for the pain.

I took the stoppered vial out of the kit that sat on the bed-table and stuck the needle in, drawing liquid into it, as instructed. I injected it into the tube port near his wrist, confident that the liquid would help him sleep. He flat-lined.

The electronic doctor substitute that had beeped calmly, ensuring his vitals were okay, went off like a horrible buzzer. I backed away from the bed, knocking against a chair, fighting a strong urge to run. I squinted at my wrinkled little sheet again to see where I had gone wrong. It wasn't my mistake. I had used the only vial in the kit, the only vial in the room. I hid in the bathroom when I heard people running down the hall. The needle kit was still sitting by the bed when they arrived but no one seemed to notice it.

They set up the heart zapper thing without much urgency. They tried three times to get him going and then shifted their positions, to try something else, I thought. When I realized that the doctor was packing it up after a token effort and a few quiet words to the nurses, I almost shouted.

After they wheeled out the corpse I wandered down the corridor like a reluctant angel of death, careful to avoid close contact with other patients.

The next time I needed to refer to the yellow sheet, I found it balled up in my fist. I went down the stairs and into the parkade across the street to a dark green Chevy that sat on its own, away from the other cars. The keys were sitting on the front left wheel. A note in the glove box gave me directions to the zoo. A few minutes into the drive Mark popped up in the backseat. Luckily he had the sense to do it at a stoplight. We both looked around to see if anyone had heard me scream.

—What happened back there? Did I kill that guy?

—You're going to have to trust me.

—I'm going to call the police.

—Do you know enough to make a good decision?

—I'm going to the police.

—Fine. I'll give you the names of our contacts there.

—Okay, forget the police. Please just tell me the truth about this organization. Ulford isn't a real corporation, is it? It doesn't really exist, does it?

—Okay, you got me. Whatever. Who cares? We just invent names to make people like you feel more comfortable with— uncertainty.

—So Ulford doesn't exist.

—Yes it does. But it won't exist three weeks from now. The name changes every month, like the password on your computer at work. If it makes you feel any better I can give you next month's name. It doesn't really matter. The name isn't important.

Raymond's knuckles are rapping at my door before the alarm has finished squawking. We drive toward the falls and park on a side street. With some soothing Mozart playing, Raymond shuts off the engine and looks at me.

—Are you sure you want to do this?

—Yes.

—You should realize that it's going to be harder to say no later on when we get down there. You'll feel pressured. There's no shame in pulling out now. You'll be in your own bed in six hours.

—Let's just get it over with.

IF YOU WERE AN ANIMAL, WHAT KIND OF ANIMAL WOULD YOU BE?

On Wednesday I was in Toronto. I smelled the sweat of the fighters as I walked into the gym, ignoring the "Closed" sign as instructed. A heavy bag near the back was still swinging.

A man in a suit stood in the middle of the ring with his hands behind his back. A guy in sweats and kickboxing gear circled the suited man, punching and kicking at his head and stomach without actually hitting him. The man in the suit grabbed the ropes, stepped down from the ring and approached me, smiling.

—You haven't told anyone about the interviews, have you? Because that would be bad. We have a policy of over-communicating here, because that minimizes confusion and strengthens unity. Everybody's eating from the same plate. That's why I'm asking you if you contacted anyone. Including your boyfriend. You might have been tempted to call him up and "check up on things" but that wouldn't be a good idea, right, "Kitten"?

He wanted to know if I would be comfortable in my sweat pants and t-shirt. There was another outfit waiting for me in the change room. When I declined, he launched into his spiel.

—The fact that you have no fighting experience is not relevant to this exercise. You will not be expected to defend yourself. You will be beaten until you are exhausted and then the exercise will begin. He won't knock you out, break your bones or make you bleed. He's very good. Any questions?

—Yes. What is Ulford?

—Ulford is an unofficial, unacknowledged group of very large corporations.

—And what does Ulford do?

—Think of your craziest conspiracy theory. Then think of a level above that. Now, any questions about the exercise?

—Can I hit back?

—Sure. But it's not going to help. It'll just tire you out.

—What's this?

—It's a mouth guard. Stick it in your mouth and bite down on it.

First thing, he punched me in the nose. He let that sink in, dancing around me as I checked for but did not find any blood. He started pushing, not hitting, just trying to wreck my balance. His feet tapped against the side of my head. Not hard hits, more like slaps stinging my skin. Every time I tried to block, his feet or fists would be hitting me in an undefended spot. I swung at him and that made him stand back and smile. While he was stationary I punched him as hard as I could in the stomach, straining something in my wrist. I tried to kick him in the balls but hit his thigh instead. He opened up his legs as if riding a horse and gestured for me to try again. I rammed my foot into his groin, hurting my instep. More smiles.

He was interested after that. I followed him around trying to hit him even though I was wheezing and thought I might puke. My arms were getting heavy, reluctant to follow orders.

He began to target the few places he had missed. A bruise for every part of my body seemed to be the plan. He hit my thighs and back, destroying my balance, making me even slower. When he came in close and tripped me, it took a long time for me to get up, even with him tapping his toes against my ribs.

I gathered myself one more time and went off, arms

windmilling as I punched and scratched until I could barely stand. I made him bleed. There were scratch marks on his forehead. He stayed just out of range after that. My lame air punches seemed to occur in slow motion compared to his jabs. He moved around me and I kept at it because I wanted to hit him one more time.

This isn't so bad. That's what I was thinking when he winded me. I fell down with my diaphragm stuck on exhale, my mouth open, sucking nothing. He held my arms out and started doing rotations with them to pump air in. As soon as I had taken a few tight breaths, he stood up and started dancing around again. Then he came down to mat level, his lips next to my ear.

—Get up. Get up or you're gonna get killed. They're coming, they're almost here. Can you hear the dogs? The dogs are almost here. Twenty feet to the car. Get up. Get up. GET UP!

I really wanted to but there wasn't a single muscle that would comply. He brought out a blanket, pulled it up to my neck and then over my face.

WHAT ARE SOME OF YOUR WEAKNESSES?

—Raymond, this need-to-know stuff is really getting to me. Can't you tell me anything about Ulford?

—What if there were an organization that was entirely oral: no offices, no documentation, no email, no registration, no corporate structure? What if there were such an organization that served as a higher level of coordination, a loose, unofficial association between a number of very large corporations that worked together to advance their common interests? Can you imagine the potential power of such an organization? If you wanted to sue that organization, how would you do it? If you wanted to write a newspaper article about it, how would you do your research? If you wanted to arrest the executive officers, nail them with million-dollar fines, how would you start that process?

—Are you saying that's what Ulford is?

—No. I just made that up. Neat idea though, don't you think?

Raymond straightens up when a white cube van pulls ahead of us. The door at the back opens and we're blinded by a rack of floodlights. Someone opens my door, the seat belt slides away and strong hands pull me gently out of the car, toward the lights, and up onto the truck. Raymond hands me a full-face motorcycle helmet with a clear visor.

—How dangerous is this?

—We make it as safe as possible.

—How many people have died doing this?

—We make it as safe as possible. You'll be fine.

It's all happening a little too fast. There are a few seconds of panicked resistance when they start to stuff me into the seat at the centre of the plastic barrel. They back away for a few moments until they sense it's safe to continue. I slide down into it on my own, allowing the crew members to tighten the straps and buckles that will hold me in place. Raymond puts his mouth to the ear-hole in my helmet.

—You're coming back. You have to. Imagine how confused Darrell would be if his wife disappeared.

The lid goes on. Through the tiny window I see someone's eye briefly, then someone's butt in blue coveralls. After a few minutes on the road we stop. I'm lifted up and tilted on my side as they carry me.

Water smacks against the barrel when I'm released. My perfectly centred weight makes the barrel roll. Through the window slit I see lights streaking past, then black water. I kick against the leg restraints, twist my neck muscles, just for a glimpse of the edge.

Going over into the noise, I buck against the straps of my electric chair and wonder if adrenaline can make your brain burst, if fright can kill you when the panic is pure.

I tumble out of the wash after about a minute or an hour of flipping and spinning. But that's behind me and now I'm ready for a moon landing. Bring it on. Feeling pretty good now, great actually, except for that popping sound and the freezing water that's starting to soak my feet.

I get to drown now. After surviving the trial I will swallow a bunch of water, my lungs will try to use it as air for a minute or so and then I'll drown.

The window in my sinking barrel is fogged over and black. It's really hard not to feel sorry for myself as I hit the bottom of the Niagara River with a thud, a few hours before dawn, with only a few insane people who know where I am but probably don't have the skill to rescue me.

With water up to my chest and my fingers almost touching the buckles, there are three knocks on the barrel. Three knocks, evenly spaced, the kind a person might make. Freezing water still creeps up the back of my neck, absorbed quickly by the foam inside the helmet as I listen for something else. A cord or rope binds against the plastic. Then more thumping and the whine of an electric motor.

One final bump and the lid comes off. They undo the straps, tip the barrel and I come splashing out with the water. From the stern deck of the boat I can see the Falls, now a half kilometre away. A techie shows me the flooding mechanism on the barrel, the plug that pops out from a burst of pressurized air. I'm tempted to hit him but he's deep into the technical genius of it, far beyond understanding my emotions.

Raymond wraps me in a blanket and walks me to the bow, away from the lights and the crew. The Falls are looking postcard pretty again, harmless.

The old guy I killed at the hospital comes up to say hi and congratulate me on completing the interview process.

—Were you scared?

—Yes, but I kept it under control.

—What about the screaming?

—I didn't scream. I'm proud of that. I didn't scream at all.

From behind, Raymond slips headphones over my ears so I can hear a one-minute segment of a woman screaming, swearing, calling out the name of someone named Darrell. I'm grateful for the railing. My jaw clamps down and I try not to think about the two men on either side of me, watching with clinical detachment.

This is probably another test: complete destruction of all personal reserves. I turn to Raymond, the prick I used to think was a nice guy. His arms open to me and he draws me in, whispering into my ear: that was hard, that was hard.

Five days back in Vancouver and the cats have finally forgiven me for my absence. In the backyard, among the rose bushes, I take a call from my bank manager. He explains that the rejection of our mortgage application had been an unfortunate mistake, a clerical error. Every second sentence is some kind of apology. He calls me Ms. Pritchard now, even though I've been plain old Susan for the last five years. Robert's voice almost seems to crack in spots. He insists on coming to our house and approving our mortgage at fifty thousand dollars more than our requested amount, two full points below the going rate.

I switch off and the phone rings immediately. I pick up, assuming it's Robert with a few apologies he forgot to make. It's the high-tech firm in North Vancouver that turned me down nine months ago. The person they hired didn't work out—as of today—and the VP wants me to come in on Monday so I can share my ideas about the future direction of the company.

As I stumble back into one of the deck chairs, Darrell wants to know what that was all about. Why am I smiling? I don't really know, I tell him, but if I had to guess I'd say that my interviews went well.